FATHER FIGURE

She opened the door to the basement. There was enough light for her to see and grab a six-pack each of Cherry Coke and 7-Up. She turned to go back to the kitchen.

The light went out.

Shelly stopped for a minute, her pulse quickening. Then she stepped into the kitchen, half-expecting to see one of her friends.

She heard a sound, turned, and saw someone in the shadows. A man, dappled by slices of moonlight.

"Dad?" she said quietly. "Is that you? I'm trying to . . ." She paused. "Dad?"

No, it's not, she seemed to hear.

Then, with a hint of amusement, she heard the man say slowly, quietly—

"I'm not Dad."

SPINE TINGLING HORROR
from Zebra Books

CHILD'S PLAY (1719, $3.50)
by Andrew Neiderman
From the day the foster children arrived, they looked up to Alex. But soon they began to act like him—right down to the icy sarcasm, terrifying smiles and evil gleams in their eyes. Oh yes, they'd do anything to please Alex.

THE DOLL (1788, $3.50)
by Josh Webster
When Gretchen cradled the doll in her arms, it told her things—secret, evil things that her sister Mary could never know about. For it hated Mary just as she did. And it knew how to get back at Mary . . . forever.

DEW CLAWS (1808, $3.50)
by Stephen Gresham
The memories Jonathan had of his Uncle and three brothers being sucked into the fetid mud of the Night Horse Swamp were starting to fade . . . only to return again. It had taken everything he loved. And now it had come back—for him.

SIGHT UNSEEN (2038, $3.95)
by Andrew Neiderman
David was a smart one; he had a gift. The power to read people's minds. To see the future. To know terrifying things. Like who would live. And who would die . . .

THE ALCHEMIST (1865, $3.95)
by Les Whitten
Of course, it was only a hobby. No harm in that. The small alchemical furnace in the basement could hardly invite suspicion. After all, Martin was a quiet, government worker with a dead-end desk job. . . . Or was he?

Available wherever paperbacks are sold, or order direct from the Publisher. Send cover price plus 50¢ per copy for mailing and handling to Zebra Books, Dept. 2121, 475 Park Avenue South, New York, N.Y. 10016. Residents of New York, New Jersey and Pennsylvania must include sales tax. DO NOT SEND CASH.

MATTHEW J. COSTELLO

SLEEP TIGHT

ZEBRA BOOKS
KENSINGTON PUBLISHING CORP.

ZEBRA BOOKS

are published by

Kensington Publishing Corp.
475 Park Avenue South
New York, NY 10016

First printing: July 1987

Printed in the United States of America

To Ann, who kept me honest; Devon, who scouted the locations; and Nora, who got me out of my office.

Prologue

It was the first really hot day of summer. Hot and humid, with a sticky heaviness in the air that made everyone feel absolutely miserable.

Tommy Burdick felt miserable. He was only seven and stuck at home while the bigger kids could walk on their own to the town pool. If he closed his eyes he could almost see the splashing and hear the constant screaming of all the kids getting nice and cool in the sparkling blue water.

Later. That's what his mother had said. Later we'll go to the pool. After your little sister wakes up. You play outside now. And be quiet. Then his mother was lost to the Donahue Show and Mr. Coffee, while he played in the miserable back yard.

But once outside, he had the beginning of an idea, which miraculously turned into a plan. A dangerous plan to be sure, but one which made his freckled face come all aglow. He'd go to the pool. By himself. He'd walk the ten or twelve blocks on his own. Without his mother knowing it.

Of course, he'd have to let her know he left. He knew, from repeated lectures, how mothers "go crazy" with worry. He knew, because his mother had become "crazy" many times. So he'd leave a note. "Gone to pool," it would say. "I will stay in shallow end."

Eventually she'd come and get him, waking the baby up for the great emergency, but by then he'd at least have had a couple of good jumps in the cool water. And who knows? After the lecture she might even decide to stay, especially if she met up with some of the other mothers. It was worth it.

His fate sealed, Tommy entered the house, letting the front door bang shut as he came in.

"Be quiet, Tommy!" his mom hissed in a strange way like some kind of barking snake. "Your sister needs more sleep."

Yeah, he nodded. She needs more sleep. She's training to be an Olympic sleeper. The only time she's awake is to eat and get her diaper changed.

He tiptoed up the stairs, past his sister's closed door, and into his own chaotic room. He snatched his bathing suit, still wet from the day before, off the floor and tucked it under his arm real tight. He printed a note and put it on his dresser against a small mound of mate-less socks.

In a moment he was outside, his heart beating quickly. He walked away from his small home and, without looking back, headed in the direction of the Harley town pool. After the first block, breathing came easier. Why, Tommy thought, it might be an hour or so before Mom noticed that her sandy-haired son was nowhere to be found.

By the third block, Tommy had begun to feel nervous about his little adventure. He knew the way,

8

sure enough. It was just that, for the first time, he was on a block that he'd never been alone on before. Alone, and unwatched.

Yet, he felt like he *was* being watched. The street was absolutely empty and the only sound was the chorus of hums from the air conditioners. None of the old people, who seemed to guard each block, were sitting on their porches this morning.

Then why, he wondered, did he feel watched? A little voice in his mind suggested going back, telling him that he'd be just in time for the unending battles of Tom and Jerry. He could hang out in front of the TV until lunch, and then go to the pool in the family's new Dodge Caravan.

But the voice faded, and he ridiculed the babyish feelings that colored this, his first really big adventure alone.

So he walked, sweating more now as he exerted himself under the hot sun, savoring even more the thought of the first splash into the pool and the instant when that exhilarating, cooling shock of water would hit his body.

Five blocks, he had counted, and halfway there now. He was tempted to run, to sprint all the way to the pool. But he didn't want to draw attention to himself, not now when he was almost there.

The feeling came again. Stronger now. He knew someone was watching him. He felt the eyes following his steps as he padded his way up the slight incline of the sidewalk. He felt caught now, as though his mother would pop out of a nearby bush and throw a net over him, dragging him back to the house, away from the cool water.

Tommy looked ahead to the corner and saw someone standing there. Standing there, and waiting. Tommy stopped now, his breathing once again becoming shallow, his fear becoming real. His mother had told him about people. People who steal children and they're never, ever seen again. Never, except in some out-of-date picture on a milk carton.

Time to end the adventure, he told himself. He could still get back now, rip up his note, and wait until his dumb sister woke up. Better that than walking past the stranger.

He turned and hurried back, his dimpled knees a bit wobbly as he tried to take larger, faster strides back home.

He glanced over his shoulder to catch a glimpse of the stranger. But he wasn't there. Gone, thought Tommy. Back into his air-conditioned house, away from the hot sidewalk. Yeah, probably just some old guy taking a little walk. Nothing to be scared of.

Tommy felt his fear ebb and he was simply hot and sticky once more. But his little trip was over. Nothing to be afraid of, he repeated, but still, he was going back home. He turned once again to continue the walk back home.

The hands closed around him quickly. One hand held him tightly around his mid-section, while the other covered his mouth. Tommy tried to scream but no sound escaped the barrier of the massive hand. His legs kicked in mid-air, sometimes landing on the stranger, but mostly churning the air. In that moment Tommy thought of the small bug he'd dropped into a wolf spider's web. He thought of the way it kicked and kicked, going nowhere while the wolf spider ambled down towards it.

Tommy could see forward, as he was dragged down a driveway between two houses. Didn't anybody see? he wondered. He twisted his head back and forth trying to look at his captor as though that would magically convince him to let Tommy go. See? his eyes would say. I'm only a small boy. You've made a mistake. You don't want me.

But Tommy was wrong there. He was just a small boy. But this had been no mistake. Tommy was the first.

And the stranger could have told him.

The first had to be a small boy.

PART I

Chapter 1

Jack Reilly sat behind a small antique desk, its oaken surface filled with invoices from book distributors, game manufacturers, and other companies that kept his small enterprise, The Book Room, running. Fortunately, he knew that his book store's accounts held more than enough to appease these seemingly endless creditors. Enough even to allow him to take his wife Julie out to dinner this Friday, no kids invited. One more grand family repast at McDonald's and he knew that he'd go McCrazy.

It was nice to be a bit ahead of the game. The wolves were no longer at the door. In fact, Jack was starting to feel faint twinges of success. His family might not be ready for the heavy-duty consuming Madison Avenue might like, but they were doing okay.

And the store just got busier and busier, to the point that Jack had given some thought to remodeling, or even expansion.

"Excuse me, Jack." The stern finger tapping on his left shoulder interrupted his capitalist reverie. He knew from the raspy, quivering voice that it was dear

Miss Waverly, a retired teacher seventy-five years young.

"Sorry to bother you, Jack, but your girl up front—sweet thing that she is—couldn't help me. I'm sure you could."

"I'll certainly try, Miss W. What's it this week? A new Barbara Cartland, or a Janet—"

The old lady shook her head. "No, it's someone new. I saw it advertised last night after the news. I think it had the word 'love' in the title."

Along with 5,000 other romance books, thought Jack.

"Let me see," he said, standing up and dwarfing his former third-grade teacher (who nonetheless still made him feel that primordial respect that a former student always has). "I know we got in *Love's Last Fling*, and *Triumph of Love*, and, er, *Love, Passion, and Tomorrow*."

Miss Waverly, never married but with a history that some described as interesting, shook her head through the entire list. "No-o-o. I'd remember the name, though, if I heard it."

"Well, why don't you check out the new paperback section and I'll make a note to keep my eyes open for it."

"Yes, you do that, and I'll go browse. Thanks, Jack."

He watched her walk away, five feet and two inches of determination and, he knew, bravery. She had borne more tragedies than most people, and yet she retained an exuberant feistiness that Jack found endearing.

"Mr. Reilly! You've got a call!" Jack's sales clerk,

plump and plain by his wife's fiat, often forgot that she could simply buzz him on his desk phone. When she yelled for him, it made him feel like he was working on the docks.

"Book order?" he called back to her as he reached for the phone.

"No, it's," and she lowered her voice to a highly amplified stage whisper, "it's the Chief of Police."

Mayor business, thought Jack. It's funny, but sometimes he forgot he was the Mayor. He didn't really feel like a mayor. But as soon as he had put his store on a relatively firm foundation, he had taken a look at the monkey show that passed for local politics in Harley. No decent parks for the kids, building projects that never got completed, and a town image that didn't exactly make Harley appear to be the jewel of the Hudson River. And having a state prison in the town certainly didn't help things, despite the pathetic attempts to turn it into a tourist attraction. Well, Jack had his store here, and his family, and no plans to move on. If he had to get involved in local politics to straighten out his town, then so be it. Besides, he liked being Mayor.

"Hi Tom. What's up?" Tom DeFalco, Police Chief in Harley for over twenty years, was someone who shared Jack's feelings for Harley. More than anyone else DeFalco felt this was *his* town.

"Jack, I waited to tell you till we were sure something really happened. Well, it turns out, er, that something has. The papers will have it tomorrow, and people are more 'n likely to call you. You know how scared people can get. . . ."

"Tom, I don't want to be blunt or anything, but

feel free to let me know just what people will be calling me about."

The Chief cleared his throat. "Oh, I'm sorry. Like I said, we weren't sure it happened. It's Tommy Burdick. You know, the family on Cullen Street right near you? Seems the boy disappeared. Gone. Vanished."

Jack sensed something then, standing by his desk in a little alcove at the rear of the store. He didn't know what it was. Only later, when everything was moving too fast, would he recognize the smell as it became clearer, stronger, and finally overpowering.

The hint of fear mingled quietly amidst the late-afternoon smell of the bookstore. For the moment it went unnoticed.

Noah's upside-down body was moving to and fro, suspended from a tire that strained a single branch of the huge maple tree.

"Daddy!" his voice screamed out. Jack, getting out of his car, wondered how Noah could be sure that the upside-down image was indeed his own pop.

Noah performed a strange sort of twisting flip to the ground and sprang up, running to his father. Jack enjoyed the welcome, even if Noah's enthusiasm threatened to knock him right over. As Jack walked toward the house, Noah dangled from his right arm.

"Bring anything, Dad? Any new books?"

"Not tonight, champ. And what did you do all day?"

"Nothing," Noah answered, his curly blond hair glowing in the rich afternoon sunlight. Such a beautiful boy, Jack thought.

"Where's Sarah?" Jack asked Noah.

"Dunno. Can I watch somethin', Dad? Please?" Noah was making what he knew to be a futile bid to watch some mindless mayhem on TV. He didn't even bother to check his father's shaking head.

By now they had reached the side door to the house, and could hear the reassuring clatter from the kitchen. Julie Reilly was putting four plates on the table. At thirty-two, she remained what she was when Jack had first met her at New York University, tall, slender, and absolutely striking. Her long blond hair—always too fine, she complained—caught each little breeze as she darted about the kitchen. Not a natural homemaker by any means, nor possessing any desire to be one, Julie preferred her hours at her potter's wheel, shaping slender vases and bowls that she'd glaze with a warm mixture of earthen colors. Her work sold well, but she always hated to part with one of her treasures just for some money. She and Jack shared the job of keeping the house running, and Julie was grateful for that.

Jack walked into the kitchen and, seeing that Noah was already nosing about elsewhere, gave his wife a kiss and a firm grab at her bottom. As usual, she let out a loud squeak, bringing Noah scrambling back to the kitchen.

Meanwhile, Jack began looking over the day's mail. "Where's Sarah?" he asked Julie casually.

"At Shelly's. They're planning some kind of pool party. Maybe this weekend, I think. Are we still on for Friday? You're not going to stand me up, buster, are you?"

Now it was Julie's turn to move closer to Jack, crumpling the mail against him. He smiled.

"Well?" she asked. "We can go parking afterwards, and who knows what might happen, if you play your cards right."

Jack looked at Julie, thinking how little they really looked at each other. Sure, they talked a lot, but somehow they just seemed to look to the side, ever so slightly, as though something bad might happen if they held each other's gaze a moment longer. Maybe there were secrets each had to guard.

He wanted to tell her.

But not now. Not with Noah running back and forth, pulling at Jack's arm, climbing onto a chair, demanding everything from peanuts to a hot fudge sundae.

And he wished Sarah would get home. He wanted everyone together, filling the house with noise, pushing away the sound of a little boy lost.

Julie was just out of the shower and toweling her hair dry. Downstairs, Sarah was watching MTV while waiting for the next breathless phonecall from one of her friends. Noah was in his room, right next door, asleep, angelic, and, for the first time today, quiet.

Jack walked into the bedroom.

"Oh!" Julie said. "You startled me. Spying on a defenseless lady fresh from the shower?"

Jack smiled weakly. "Something bad happened today, Julie. It will be in the papers tomorrow."

Julie's face shifted, concern filling it instantly.

"Bad? To you?"

"Tommy Burdick disappeared."

He had her attention now. All the magazine articles on "lost" children, the television documentaries, the children's pictures posted in shop windows, all of that came real close now. Julie sat down, her wet hair forgotten. The Burdicks were no friends of theirs, to be sure. Mr. Burdick had been living downtown recently, and Julie rarely saw his wife. Not even neighbors, really. Still, she knew the freckled face of little Tommy. And, worse, she could imagine what might be happening to it.

"Oh, God," she said quietly. And then she listened as Jack told her the small amount of information that the police had. When he was done, Julie asked the same question that Jack had asked Tom DeFalco.

"Could it have been Mr. Burdick? I mean, he's been pretty upset lately. Karen Whately told me that he drove to the house last Saturday night and started screaming at his wife. Could he have . . ."

"Maybe. They couldn't find him this afternoon. It's his day off from the GM plant. He could be anywhere. Sure, he's suspect. I'm sure everyone hopes that it is him. I mean, that's understandable. But Julie," Jack said sitting down next to Julie, hearing the cicadas outside rattle their night song, "just keep Noah where you can see him."

"But I always . . ."

"I know, I know. Just, hell, don't even go inside for a phone call, or a fresh cup of coffee, and leave him out!"

Julie's blue eyes flashed.

"You're a fine one to talk. Sometimes I don't think

21

you know where Noah is even when you're watching him."

Jack stood up. "Hey, I didn't want to start a battle over this, it's just . . ."

"Mommy . . . Mommy!"

Julie looked stonily at Jack. "There, you woke him up." And she moved now to soothe her Noah back to safe slumber, leaving Jack alone with the darkness he had brought home.

Eddie Dixon, standing next to Fredo's Portuguese-American Deli on Main Street, mopped his brow with an already wet cloth.

Shit!, he thought. This little pisshole of a town is hot. Too damn hot to move. Almost too hot to drink, the way the booze makes you feel kinda warm all over. Too hot to do anything but watch all the cars drive right past the center of town, without so much as a glance at old Eddie D.

Harley-on-Hudson. It's not really a town, Eddie thought. It's just a prison with some shops around, surrounded by the shitty little houses of the people who couldn't afford to live in one of the good river towns. A prison town, home to the Harley Correctional Facility, nothing more. And if there was one thing Eddie knew, it was the four walls of the prison itself.

Fifteen long fuckin' years, baking in the summer, freezing in the winter. Watching the stinking Hudson River through iron bars, seeing the glow of New York City at night like some great neon sign selling something that he'd never be able to buy. No food worth eating, and no pussy at all. Fifteen years because a little robbery got fucked up and Eddie punked out with his gun and blew a bald-headed fucker away.

And Eddie dug it, dug seeing the guy's fancy robe dotted with big blobs of red and tiny specks of white. It was the best thing he ever saw, better even than in the movies. But it cost him. Fifteen years watching sailboats and chunks of ice move down the fuckin' river.

Here he was, back in Harley, watching everyone drive past the dead stores on Main Street, hustling their station wagons to and from the train station, working their asses off for the day they could buy their way out of Harley and into a real town, a town without a prison.

And old Eddie was back watching them, thinking about what he was going to do, just killing time in Harley. His eyes followed the slope of the hill down to the train station, and he laughed as he looked beyond it.

Here he was again looking at the fuckin' river.

Only this time there were no bars, no walls, and no prison.

Chapter 2

She knew it was a dream.

The muted colors, the feeling that time had stopped and moving images could freeze into a still life, and the hollow sounds that filled this world all told Julie that it was a dream. And for now she luxuriated in it, and the warm feelings it brought her sleeping mind.

They were outside, in front of their small Tudor-style home. Noah was standing on the lawn, right near the sidewalk, looking up at Julie, who was near the porch. He was smiling, his eyes saying, "I love you, and I know that you love me." His face caught the warm glow of the setting sun.

Sarah came out of the house, full of energy, smiling as she passed Julie, and time started again. Julie smelled her daughter's newly washed hair, laced with just a hint of perfume sneaked from Mom's dresser.

Noah and Sarah stood together, and Sarah held Noah's hand tightly. Julie's heart was filled with such a feeling of love that if she were awake she'd be crying. So wonderful, her mind whispered, so beautiful . . . .

But then they stepped off the lawn onto the sidewalk, grinning at each other as they did it, and Julie's sleeping body twitched slightly. "No," she tried to say. "Back on the lawn where you belong!" But, of course, no sound came out of her mouth. It's that old trick of dreamland, thought Julie. You get to be in the movie, to be the star even, but the script is under someone else's control.

The children were smiling, happy, and laughing at Julie's attempt to say something. The wind picked up and leaves started to fall, swirling around in little spirals at the children's feet. The sun was gone, masked by dirty gray clouds. Julie knew this wasn't real; she knew that she was asleep. But she also knew that her dream had just changed into a nightmare.

She tried to move as the wind buffeted her. Julie had to get the children and bring them inside now, before it got dark. The children just looked at their mom, laughing as Julie moved ever so slowly toward them. Moving to her children was the hardest thing that she had ever done.

Then it was dark. Bluish moonlight outlined Noah and Sarah.

"Please," she said in her dream. "I'm almost there. Let me save them!"

But of course she was too late. The man appeared from nowhere. Tall, slender, and wearing a wide-brimmed hat that shaded his face. But his hand was visible, grabbing each of the children and dragging them backward.

Julie could hear their screams and her muscles strained against whatever was holding her back. She looked down and saw them—people, grinning wildly, holding her legs and arms and head. Holding her rock hard. Not allowing her to follow but forcing her to watch, the utter hopeless horror of it crushing her.

"Jack," she whimpered, wondering where he could be. "Jack. Oh God, please help us."

Then somehow she was screaming in her dream. "Jack! Jack!" And the hands let go, and the people disappeared, and she woke up.

Whispering, "Jack . . ." She was sitting up, and sweat was running down her body.

Jack slept on. Julie's heart still thundered, even as the normalcy of the bedroom returned. The crumpled pile of clothes on the floor, the gentle ticking of the Regulator clock downstairs, a snort from Noah—who always made sounds in his sleep.

The nightmare was over. Jack was here.

Julie thought of checking the kids, or getting a drink of water. But she simply lay down and pulled herself close to Jack's warm body.

For tonight, the show was over.

Chief DeFalco opened the door to the patrol car and slid next to Officer Allan Smith.

"Morning, sir," Smith said sharply.

"Morning, Allan," DeFalco answered. He liked Smith. The black officer, only the second on Harley's small force, was sharp and professional. And DeFalco knew all too well the kind of trouble a black officer like Smith often had to deal with.

"They have Burdick at the house now, sir, and they've already started to check his story."

"Good. Put the light on, will you? See if we can't slice through some of this traffic. It seems like they're always ripping up the road for some damn thing or another."

Smith turned on the overhead emergency lights and, with judicious squawks from the siren, was able to cut through the single-lane traffic. Within minutes they were in front of the Burdicks' small house, a weather-beaten Cape Cod shaded by a huge white pine tree. DeFalco was out of the car before the engine was off.

He moved quickly up the front steps to the door and entered the house. An uncomfortable tableau awaited him.

Mr. and Mrs. Burdick sat on opposite sides of the tiny living room with two policemen standing in the middle. DeFalco felt the heavy atmosphere in the room, the product of yelling and crying that, with luck, was all over now.

He gave a nod to one of the policemen, a sergeant, who ran over and handed DeFalco a small notebook.

"Hmm. Okay. Yeah." DeFalco muttered aloud as the sergeant whispered in his ear. "Okay. Now, Mrs. Burdick," DeFalco said, turning gently toward Tommy's mother, "I know this is very painful for you. I understand that. But if we're going to help get Tommy back we'll need your help."

"Stupid bitch."

DeFalco looked over at Mr. Burdick, whose hand cradled a glass. From the looks of things, it wasn't Mr. Burdick's first drink of the morning.

"Er, Mr. Burdick," DeFalco said, turning toward the man. "I'll need your help too. If you can just be

28

patient, I'd like to—"

"She's a stupid bitch." Burdick stood up and pointed a beefy finger at his wife. "It's her damn fault Tommy's gone. Watching her stupid TV all day and—"

Mrs. Burdick meanwhile burst into tears. A crumpled napkin was twisted, almost woven, around her fingers. DeFalco saw a toddler standing in a playpen in the dining room, looking on stoically, thoroughly nonplussed. Hang in there, kid, DeFalco said to himself. It's going to be a bumpy ride.

"Mr. Burdick, we can talk about this at the station if you don't let me ask questions here. Now please. Sit down." DeFalco looked right at Burdick. It was a look that not many ignored. Burdick sat down heavily, and the leatherette chair gave out a windy sigh.

DeFalco turned back to Mrs. Burdick, gentle once more.

"I know that you told these officers everything yesterday. Could we please go over it one more time?"

Mrs. Burdick looked up, knowing that she was on call again to tell the story for the fourth time. Eventually, as neighbors and friends spoke to her, she'd lose count of the number of repetitions.

"Tommy wanted to go to the pool," she said slowly. "But Tammy here had just gone in for her nap. So I said, 'No, Tom. We'll go later. After your sister wakes up.' It was real hot yesterday. I was doing dishes, cleaning up . . ."

"Watching the fucking tube," Mr. Burdick muttered, and DeFalco quickly shot him a warning glance. Mrs. Burdick continued.

29

"At about ten-thirty I checked on Tommy. He usually plays in the back or rides his bike out front. I called for him, but he didn't come. I started getting scared. So I went up to his room, and I found this."

She handed the note, obviously crumpled and then straightened out, to DeFalco.

GONE TO POOL. I WILL STAY IN SHALLO END. TOMMY

"Did you find it crumpled like this?"

Mrs. Burdick shook her head. "No. I . . . got angry."

"Then you did what?"

"I woke Tammy. Her diaper needed changing, so I changed her and then got the stroller and . . . and . . ."

Mrs. Burdick began crying full-out now, and even her husband seemed affected. He raised his glass to his lips and sucked it dry.

DeFalco moved to the couch and sat next to Mrs. Burdick, touching her shoulder gently, trying somehow to calm her down.

"There, there. Okay. We're almost done. So you followed the way to . . ."

"Yes, I went the way Tommy would go. I . . . I thought he'd be in the pool. I was going to scold him . . . tell him how scared I was. But when I got there, he wasn't in the pool. The man at the gate said that Tommy had never arrived. . . . He never even got to the pool. I . . . I . . . Oh, God! Where's my baby?" She howled now, a creature trapped by her loss. "You'll find my baby, won't you? Please. Tell me it will be okay. Tell me."

She melted into him now, and DeFalco knew why he had stayed in his job. Various security services had tried to hire him away, offering much more money to protect their corporate clients. But sitting here, knowing that it was up to him to somehow help this woman—well, DeFalco thought, you don't get more needed than that.

"Billy," the Police Chief said to the sergeant. "You got a map of the suspected route, right?"

"Yeah, Tom. We've also got statements from people at the pool."

DeFalco nodded to the sergeant to come and take his place next to Mrs. Burdick. Seeing her husband fix another drink, he decided to get at the father before he was too drunk. For a moment Mrs. Burdick sat rigidly when DeFalco stood up, but then the sergeant was next to her, a warm body somehow soothing the grief that twisted her insides like a rubber band.

DeFalco went and stood next to Tommy's father.

"Mr. Burdick, you've told my officers that you were fishing upstate yesterday."

"Yes," Burdick said, subdued now that he was being questioned. DeFalco flipped through the small notebook he had been handed. "With a Gary Jenks, right?"

"Yes. Since I moved out of the house, I've been using my days off to fish. When we go to court, and I get a regular visiting schedule, then I guess I'll see the kids. . . ."

"Mr. Burdick, have you ever threatened to steal Tommy away?"

"Hell, no."

31

"But didn't you drive up here last Friday and start shouting at the house about how you were going to take the children?"

"Okay. Look, I had been drinking and, let's face it, I'm pretty upset living downtown and all. This is my house, my kids, and I love them. But I know that they belong in their house with their mother, even if she doesn't take such good care of them."

"Shut the hell up, you!" Mrs. Burdick screamed, rising from the shelter of the sergeant's shoulder. DeFalco nodded to the sergeant to gently guide the woman down again.

"Please, Mr. Burdick," DeFalco said calmly. "This is difficult enough as it is."

The man took a sip from his drink. "Yeah. Look, just find my kid, will you? He isn't here and I don't got him. And every minute you spend talking to me is another mile farther away he could be."

At that moment Officer Smith entered the house, and both parents turned to look at him, searching for some sign that the pain was over. But Smith's face was all business as he handed DeFalco a note.

"Okay," the Chief said. "Thanks. Well, Mr. Burdick, Mr. Jenks has corroborated your story. One thing I'd like to ask you, though, before you go. Is there anybody either of you know who might have something against you, or maybe someone who particularly liked your little boy? A friend, a relative, anyone?"

For the first time that morning, the estranged couple looked at each other and, almost in unison, shook their heads.

"Thank you," DeFalco said quietly. "Rest assured

we'll be doing everything we can. I've already given the State Police the photos you gave me, and by this afternoon they'll be at every police station in the state. Also by this afternoon, they'll be all over the country. Sergeant Rolston will be your contact. You can call him any time you want, and he'll let you know when we have news about Tommy."

That is, DeFalco thought grimly, if we get news. And if there is any news, Mr. and Mrs. Burdick may just find it the most horrible news that they ever heard.

Chief DeFalco left the house quickly, eager to stand outside and breathe a few moments before getting back into the patrol car.

Jack was behind the counter of The Book Room when Sarah walked into the store with the proprietary air of someone who knew the owner well.

"Hi Dad," she said cheerfully while scanning the magazine rack.

"Well, to what do I owe the honor, my dear? I haven't seen you in here since last . . ."

"Inventory," Sarah added. "Yeah, that kinda put me off books and book stores, if you know what I mean. I like books all right, but counting them is not my idea of a great time."

Jack laughed. "Nor mine. But hey, you got paid for it, right?"

Sarah nodded, and Jack marveled at how fast she was growing up. Kindergarten wasn't that long ago, and here she was, tan, trim, and ready for the frantic social life of the sixth grade. Already boys were calling up for dates, setting off an alarm in Jack from somewhere in his mind he didn't even know about. Lately, he'd been skimming the adolescent section of his psychology shelves, storing up ammunition for the battles he knew would eventually come.

"Sort of quiet today, ain't it, Dad?"

"You missed the big lunch-hour crush. Everybody's at the pool. Speaking of which, why aren't you there?"

Sarah walked behind the counter, sidling up next to her father. Jack immediately braced himself for the pitch he knew was coming.

"I'm going later," Sarah said casually. "But I wanted to talk to you. You see, there's this pool party this Saturday night. Shelly's having it. There'll be a barbecue and music and—"

"Boys?"

"Dad! Can I finish, please?" Sarah's exaggerated sternness gave her the momentary advantage. "Anyway, yes there'll be boys. But tons of adult supervision, tons! And here's the best part. After the party, Shelly's having a sleep-over. Isn't that great?"

"Great," Jack mumbled. "You want the keys to the car?"

"Dad-dy!" Sarah said, letting the last syllable plummet two octaves in total annoyance.

"What did your Mom say?" Jack asked, trying to get negotiations started again. It wouldn't take too much to get Sarah storming out of the store in a major pout.

"She said it's up to you. She thought that it was kinda okay."

Up to me, Jack thought. People don't know

34

responsibility until they have kids. And then that's about all they do know. Disaster lurks around every corner and you can only pray that you say and do the right thing to get the infant to adulthood without a major calamity.

They were interrupted by the newsboy bringing in his copy of *The Harley Courier*. It flopped open to the headline:

7-YEAR-OLD DISAPPEARS

It made Tommy Burdick sound like the invisible boy, Jack thought. Here today, gone . . .

"Well?" Sarah's blue eyes were aimed right at Jack, weapons of some potency.

"Sorry, sweatheart, I was looking at the headline. Well, my answer is 'yes' to the pool party and a big fat 'maybe' to the sleep-over. I want to talk to Shelly's mom before I give the official okay."

"But all the other kids can—"

"Yeah, but you're not all the other kids. Say, as long as you're here, want to earn some cash? You can help finance your next fall's wardrobe. There's some books—"

"No thanks, Dad. I'm meeting everyone at the pool in a little while. Will you check on the sleep-over tonight. You will? Great. Bye Dad."

And with a quick peck at Jack's cheek, Sarah darted away, bursting with excitement, energy, and just enough independence to scare Jack.

He picked up the paper and read the article about Tommy Burdick, letting the newsprint make the story seem as though it were about someone he'd

35

never heard of.

The heat of the day didn't dissipate at night. In fact, it seemed to get even hotter. The air was full of moisture, and a steamy haziness filled the streets even as the sun went down. Air conditioners were pumping away full force on all the blocks, creating little islands of relief while making even more heat in their exhaust.

St. Paul's Episcopal Church was not air-conditioned, nor was it likely to ever be air-conditioned. And, as Helen Waverly had informed a fellow member of the church choir just this night, it was "one damned hot place" in the summer. Of course, in the winter, it let in every cold draft from every direction, but that was no consolation now. And, with church attendance way down, any major renovations were only dreams.

The talk before this evening's choir practice had been about the missing boy. The choir director, a plump woman with an eternally pleasant outlook on life, had turned uncharacteristically solemn as she asked everyone to lower their heads and pray. Helen had prayed, knowing well the pain of a sudden, tragic loss. As she prayed she thought, not of Tommy, but instead of her family's house burning, while she heard the screams of her trapped brothers and sisters. Her mother had carried her out and was about to go in for the rest of the family. But they had stopped her from going back in, the firemen seeing the utter hopelessness of getting anybody out of a house totally aflame. She had stood there, watching the feeble efforts to put out the fire, her eyes reflecting the flashing yellow and orange of the fire.

Helen had escaped, and so had her mother. But her mother had slipped into a land of sorrow that excluded Helen. Loss like that lets you know what the price of being human is. Only people can feel pain that intense and still go on living. So Helen prayed for Tommy as she thought about her family.

Choir practice was subdued. The traditional "Old 40" hymns were sung even more drearily than usual, and the newer songs, designed for guitar, tambourines, and hand clapping, were performed perfunctorily. All these good people, thought Helen, empathize with sorrow almost too easily.

Practice ended about ten minutes early. As usual, Helen declined offers of a ride home, and she wasted no time starting the eight-block walk back to her house. She'd been independent all her life, and she wasn't about to start giving that up until she had to. Besides, she usually enjoyed the walk.

But not tonight.

Too hot, for one thing, and too hazy. The cars that passed her were always going so fast, it seemed, appearing out of the dark suddenly, their headlights creating a glowing fog in the street.

After two blocks she wished she had taken a ride. It was almost unhealthy outside. When she reached the one block that had a steep incline, she was breathing heavily, trying to gulp in the thick, humid air.

She remembered that she had no book to read tonight. She had been hoping to pick up that new novel from Jack Reilly. Her romances were something she loved. They took her away, to strange places and handsome men. Through them, she became young again, beautiful, desired. . . .

She stopped.

There was something behind her. She turned just as she felt the strong hands grab her.

She opened her mouth to scream, not even knowing what her scream would sound like. But she never heard it. His hand, a massive, powerful hand, closed around her mouth, while his other hand reached around her mid-section. She felt herself being lifted up, her feet were off the ground, and then Helen began to wet herself.

Oh sweet Jesus, she thought. What is happening? Surely someone will see, someone walking a dog, or some teenagers in a car, someone.

Please, she begged silently.

But the stranger just dragged her along, down a narrow driveway between two houses. Helen turned her head, and saw the light from the windows on either side. Someone must see. They have to see.

He brought her to the back door, and she knew she was alone. No one to help, no benevolent God to grant her this one, all-important favor. She started to fight.

She brought her leg up, searching for his groin, her knee jabbing, trying to cause pain. She forced her jaw open and then tried to catch the flesh of his fingers between her teeth, but she only managed to scrape the surface.

She twisted and turned, amazingly powerful for someone her age, her anger rising and, for a moment, taking away the fear that had her pulse racing.

It changed nothing. Inexorably, the stranger

kicked open the back door and carried her through. He then kicked it shut with a bang that sounded like the end of it all.

Now fear claimed her again, causing her skin to go cold, and her eyes rolled around seeking something that would end this dream. Her muffled moans sounded like the distant bleating of some doomed animal.

The stranger dragged her down into the basement, and the rancid smell and the metallic taste in Helen's mouth told her that this was no dream.

Then, sweet God, she heard voices. Three, maybe four people. Coming from downstairs. And she sucked in the air through her nostrils thinking that this was help at last. In a minute she'd be free.

But when she saw the faces that went with the voices, Helen Waverly began to cry like a little girl.

It was Tuesday, and she was the second.

Chapter 3

Jack Reilly saw the police car slide into a vacant lot in front of his store. He watched Tom DeFalco get out of the car and walk up to the door. And as he watched Jack knew that something bad was coming.

A soft electronic bleep signaled the door opening, and Jack found that he'd walked over to meet the Police Chief.

"Good morning, Tom. I take it you don't have good news."

DeFalco nodded. He glanced at the few customers milling about. "Can you take a few minutes, Jack? Go for a short ride . . . let me talk to you a bit?"

Jack sensed the unease in DeFalco.

"Sure. Just let me tell Emily." Jack smiled weakly. "I'm sure she can hold down the fort for a little while." DeFalco watched Jack walk over to Emily, who bit her lip anxiously at the news of her new, temporary responsibilities. Then, they walked out to DeFalco's car. As Jack got in the car the radio was spewing forth an odd mixture of hiss and unintelligible conversation. Jack pushed back into his seat and felt the heavy wire mesh that separated the front and back seats. DeFalco started the engine and drove out of the shopping center.

"What's up, Tom? Any news of Tommy Burdick?" DeFalco seemed to Jack to be taking an unusual interest in driving, as though there was something he wanted to say but he had to work his courage up first.

"Nothing. Mr. Burdick's clean. We're sure of that. I have someone down at the prison, checking the records of recently released prisoners. So far they've turned up nothing. We've got pictures all over the state."

Jack saw that they were headed towards the new police station. It was a sleek, modern building. But lots of people, including the local paper, had criticized the town for building it so far from where the real "action" is. Behind the station was one of the last pieces of wild, undeveloped land in Harley. Fronted by the sprawling recycling dump, this unnamed park of towering pines was a small, gloomy place. "Development" was just around the corner.

"Where are we going?" Jack asked.

"Back here," DeFalco said as he passed the station. He parked where the road ended and the woods began. In front of the car were the enormous dumpsters, one each for recycling the differently colored glass bottles—clear, green, and brown. You could do a quick survey of current beer and wine taste in Harley just by scanning the top layer of each pile.

Jack got out and followed DeFalco, who was already walking past the dumpsters, past the faded sign that said, "Please Sort Your Bottles," into the darkness of the park. And then Jack realized that something really ghastly might be coming, something that he might not want to see.

The TV news at night—the evening horror show, as he called it—would often show pictures of a half-submerged body, a torn jacket, and, the classic image, a sopping, mud-stained teddy bear. But that was TV, the cool medium. And now a word from our sponsor.

This was real. This was life. And Jack didn't know whether he could stomach what was coming.

He ran and caught up to DeFalco.

"Hey, Tom, wait a minute. I'm not sure I want to see . . ."

DeFalco stopped, and for the first time today he faced Jack. "There's nothing to see, Mr. Mayor. Nothing except these old trees, that little stream over there. But there's something I got to tell you, just you for now. And this is as good a spot as any." He paused, dug a cigarette out of his shirt pocket, and lit it. A puff of blue smoke hung over their heads.

"I came to Harley nearly twenty-three years ago expecting, I guess, to have a quiet job in a quiet town. Things were starting to fall apart back then, with riots and protests, and I wanted to do my bit to hold them together.

"I'd been working for a year when it happened. A little girl, Susan Devlin, six, maybe seven years old . . . I forget. Anyway, she disappeared. We found no leads anywhere. She just vanished on a spring afternoon while playing outside her house. A couple of weeks later, another child, a boy, was gone. Y'know, this was way before the milk cartons had pictures with toll-free hot lines. We found nothing.

43

The whole time the paper went on about how backward and ineffective the police department was.''

DeFalco sucked at his cigarette, and he looked around as though he was seeing the woods as it once was.

"I finally found them. Here. It was a big chunk of land then, without the cheapjack condos surrounding it."

"What made you come up here?"

DeFalco shook his head.

"A hunch. I dunno. I guess I sort of wondered where would I go if I snatched a kid and wanted to hide. So I came here. Off hours."

Now DeFalco started walking again, and Jack had the eerie feeling that they were retracing steps taken over twenty years ago.

"I zigzagged. It was spring, but there's not much color on the ground under pine trees. No light gets through and the soil becomes too acid from the needles. I went back and forth, looking for a piece of color. I saw a beer can, some gum wrappers. Then, by the stream, just about there . . ."

Jack looked away to where DeFalco pointed. He saw the narrow stream and the outcrop of rock that it meandered around.

"There I saw a body. I found the girl first. Further along, I found the boy. I threw up, my stomach heaving until there was nothing left. Then I cried. Must've sat by that little boy for half an hour, wishing to God that the little body would go away."

DeFalco turned from the stream and started back to

the car.

"And the murderer?" Jack asked, his voice a whisper.

"Local fellow. Worked in the lumber yard. We found footprints, from workboots. Then someone came up with an I.D. of a car parked up near the old entrance to Route 9-A. The guy's still in some nuthouse somewhere, eating good meals, watching the Cosby Show, sleeping in a nice bed. I think if I had got to him I would have strangled the bastard. Sometimes I dream about it."

A tiny shaft of sunlight spiked through an opening in the pine canopy, hitting DeFalco's face. A spot glistened there, moist and round, and Reilly knew that DeFalco was struggling for control.

"So why did you want me here, Tom? What do you want to say?"

DeFalco stopped, rubbed his eyes quickly, and put his hand on Jack's shoulder. "For weeks the town went crazy, Jack. Every nutty idea from vigilante groups to hiring special detectives was tried. Special town meetings were held. Real circuses they were, with the police and the people screaming at each other. It was about as ugly as things can get."

Reilly nodded, chilled in the deep afternoon shade, beginning to understand where all this was headed.

"It's going to start again, Jack. Last night Helen Waverly didn't make it home from choir practice. A neighbor called us when Helen didn't drop over for her morning tea. We broke into the house. It was empty and there's no sign of Helen Waverly. Two days, two people gone. By the time tonight's paper hits the streets this town is going to be crazy

45

with fear."

DeFalco turned and walked up to his car. "It's going to become a crazy town, Jack, with frightened, crazy people. It's your town, your people."

They arrived at the car and DeFalco opened his door.

"And all I can tell you is that there's no bodies hidden in this park this time."

"We built this city. We built this city on rock-and-roll! We built this city. . . ."

My, thought Julie, the more things change, the more they stay the same. Grace Slick's still reigning queen of rock. Julie had actually missed Queen Grace's first reign, though everybody knew the quickly dated exhortation "Feed Your Head." By the time Julie was in college, her generation was worried about feeding their bods (plus finding a down payment for a Mercedes).

And here she was fixing chicken-cutlet surprise while her daughter tested the structural strength of their home with Jack's megawatt stereo and digitalized Jefferson Starship.

She took a sip of Diet Coke and tipped her can in a silent toast to longevity. She was still deciding what kind of sauce to surprise the cutlets with when the song ended and Sarah bounced into the kitchen. Her long, straight hair, a deep, lustrous brown, bounced with her.

"Where's Noah?" she asked eyeing the meal preparations and noting the unusually peaceful atmosphere in the kitchen.

"At Sam's house. I've got to pick him up in ten minutes."

Sarah slid next to her mother, and began to stir up the sauce. "What's this?" asked Julie. "Helping in the kitchen? It's not my birthday, you know."

Sarah made a face. Sarcasm went over poorly with her, Julie knew. But sometimes it was just too hard to resist.

"Mom! C'mon. You know I like to help. I'm just always so busy."

Sure, thought Julie as she waited for the next development. A few minutes went by and then . . .

"Mom." Sarah knew that her mother was indeed waiting for something. Still, surprise wasn't everything. "Mom, did you talk to Dad about this Saturday? The pool party, the sleep-over? Did you?"

"No. We haven't talked about it, Sarah. Pass me the sauce, please. Er, maybe tonight. You say that Shelly's folks will both be there?"

"Yeah. And you know how great the Jaffes are."

Right, thought Julie. She also knew how Mr. Jaffe liked to make passes at her. Blunt, clumsy things that left no doubt about their ultimate objective. And that made Julie think of something else, something dark that she didn't want to think about. Something that she had tried to forget even as it continued to dance in her head. Maybe it's me, she thought. Maybe I'm sending off some kind of message. Can people just look at me and tell that I'm dissatisfied?

"Mom! When will you talk about it?"

"Tonight, honey. Just as soon as Noah is in bed, Daddy and I will sit down and . . ."

"Great. Love you Mom." Sarah leaned up to her

47

mother, kissed her, and dashed away. "Oops," she said stopping abruptly, and she darted back to return the fork to the counter top. Then she was gone, and the Starship blasted off again.

It's so nice to have someone to help with the cooking, Julie thought wryly.

The long walk up the hill left Eddie Dixon winded. Sure he had worked out with weights in prison, shaping his arms and chest into something rock solid. But he didn't go in for any of that faggoty jogging shit. And walking from downtown to the upper, suburban hills of Harley was a bitch of a climb.

Not only that, but he was getting looks as he entered the better section of Harley. He still didn't have a lot of clothes to wear, and what he did have looked like garbage. Ragged jeans and a T-shirt sent alarms off in some people's heads.

He picked up his pace, trying to act as though he was headed someplace. Maybe to pick up his car at that gas station there, or maybe, and here he smiled, to open an account at that bank on the corner. Hell, he sure could use one of those "Open Sesame" money cards.

Anything, just as long as he didn't look like he was some punk just out of prison looking for the easiest house to crack. Some nice-looking place with no alarms, no dogs, just some doors and windows he could pry open, scooping up some goodies and then splitting downtown.

But that's not all. This town owed him. If he could

give it a bit of grief before he left, well, that would be all the better.

He was at the top of the hill when he saw a cop car coming down. Nice and cool, Eddie, he thought. Just keep walking nice and steady. I got business up here, officer. Why, sure I do.

The car slowed and Eddie felt the cop's stare, and his clothes and face were sucked into the pig's memory.

No problem, thought Eddie. I haven't done anything. Not a thing.

Not yet, anyway.

Chapter 4

Julie knelt on the bed, astride Jack, letting the sensation linger just a moment before she would shudder and it would end. The moonlight outlined her body, dabbing her with patches of gray, while Jack remained in the shadow. For the moment he was her phantom lover, a bit of everyone she had ever looked at twice. Then, he was one person in particular. Instantly she tried to push the image away, but then she let it come, filling her with an even greater excitement.

She moaned, and Jack reached out for her breasts, squeezing, caressing, tracing erratic circles around her nipples. Her eyes were closed now, and she was lost to her fantasy. Even as she remembered she told herself: she hadn't wanted the affair to happen.

But then, she asked herself, if that's true, why did it happen?

She would replay that first day many times, that exciting, titillating first brush with illicit romance and disaster, inside her head like some cherished home movie, over and over, trying to see exactly where she took that first step.

Of course, Jack had had his role to play. He had seen that, despite their best intentions, Julie was feeling trapped by the house and the all-encompassing suburban lifestyle. Despite their efforts to be above it all, to be pointedly different, it was there. Suburbia.

Inexorable fate, Julie would jokingly call it. And Jack would laugh too.

But still, he was out of the house, doing what he loved to do. No matter how much they tried to structure their lives differently, she *was* the housewife, the cook, the "primary caretaker" for their children.

Sooner or later, it would drive her nuts.

So when Jack encouraged her to set up a studio in the basement and try and spend some time on her pottery and sculpture, she jumped at the chance.

Those were exciting days, cleaning out the garbage from the basement, putting up shelves, shopping around for a good, solid work table, something hardy enough to stand being slapped by a thirty-pound block of clay.

And then the work began, tentative at first. She started by copying some of her earlier pieces done in art school.

Then, as children and home became less important, Julie's work came into its own. Her pieces were distinct, immediately striking to even the most untrained eye. She knew she was good.

Which led her to call Patrick Caldwell.

Caldwell's Hudson Gallery was the only show in

town, the only place for a local artist to exhibit his or her work in conditions close to that found in a New York gallery. It had an excellent reputation for discovering new talent, talent that was often snatched up by the colorful parade of gallery owners and buyers that trooped up the river to any Hudson Gallery opening.

She called the gallery one overcast and icy day in January, and she was shocked to find herself speaking directly with Caldwell. Yes, he told her, he'd be delighted to see some samples of her work. Perhaps a few pieces and transparencies, of course. Caldwell suggested that coming Wednesday for an appointment.

Julie was beside herself with excitement. She spent the next two days trying to decide which two or three pieces to bring, settling at last on a platter that caught the eye with its dizzying swirl of glazes, a pair of goblets, and a free-form piece, made up of smooth curves and crevices, that represented the kind of work she really wanted to do.

Julie had arranged for a sitter to watch the kids, and she arrived for her meeting a good fifteen minutes early. She spent the time strolling through the gallery, scrutinizing the work on display, feeling ever more inadequate as the appointment time grew closer.

"Mr. Caldwell will see you now," his thin-lipped receptionist finally said, and Julie met the man who was to take her life and twist it out of recognition.

He smiled as she entered, gesturing to a chair facing his desk.

"I'm very glad you could bring some of your work

to me," Caldwell said, and Julie believed him.

She talked too fast, of course, pulling her pieces out of a large case, rushing through her presentation, quickly flipping open a book of transparencies. But Caldwell took his time, examining each piece, letting his fingers run over their textured curves.

And Julie noticed something else.

He was examining her too. In between educated questions about glazes and clay mixtures, Caldwell was looking right at her, his blue eyes appraising her even as they talked of art and prices.

When he finally said, "Yes, Julie, I want to display your work," his hand reached across and covered hers in a reassuring way.

She didn't know what thrilled her more. The acceptance of her work, or the attention of a very attractive man.

They made plans for another meeting to discuss possible dates for her show, a lunch meeting at the elegant River Hill Restaurant. Julie looked forward to the luncheon in a way that made her feel positively adolescent.

Jack was happy for her. And so proud, he said. Julie knew he was relieved that she had something to take away her suburban malaise.

But, for the first time, she held something back from him. A small part of her day was held secret. Caldwell's glances, his touching of her hand, her excitement about seeing him again. A small part kept hidden, that would grow until she felt it reach every part of her life.

At first, she was disappointed with the luncheon. It was all about price points, and deadlines, and, of course, the number of pieces to be displayed. But later, as they ate, she felt Caldwell's attention shift, and she became his focus as she talked to him about her days at NYU, her family, her thoughts. She felt a warm glow, something vaguely remembered from earlier days.

I'm married, with kids, she told herself.

But the pull of the fantasy was too strong.

The next time they met, it was in his office, supposedly to look over her newer work. It was lunch time. The building was closed, the receptionist away, and Caldwell closed his office door. He talked, and circled her until she felt she'd go crazy with anticipation. He touched her shoulder, and let his hand caress her face. Then they attacked each other, removing their clothes with a giddy abandon.

They made love on the polished oak desk.

It was good, very good. Liberating. So much so that Julie's guilt did not arrive till much, much later.

That too would grow.

"Wait," Jack whispered. "I hear something."

Julie stopped moving, and listened. Then she heard the creaking sound from the bedroom floor.

"Mommy . . . Mom?" It was Noah, at their door, and all of their switches clicked off as they shifted back to being parents.

"Honey," Julie called, wondering why she hadn't heard the door open. "What's wrong?"

Noah stood there, at the threshold, his blue and red Superman pajamas making him look like a midget avenger coming to prevent the dastardly deed from reaching completion. In his hand was his trusty stuffed monkey, whose bedraggled body and confused expression seemed to protest this late-night escapade.

"I'm scared, Mommy." Julie could feel Jack pulling out of her, and she slid off. She didn't bother gathering up her nightgown. Noah had seen both of his parents naked many times.

She went over to him and picked him up, her voice gentle in his ear. She carried him back to his bed, and sat beside him in the deep darkness of his small room.

"Mommy, I'm still scared."

"It was just a dream, Noah. And dreams aren't—"

"There was this man. And he was coming inside our house. And I couldn't run away. I really couldn't." Noah's voice grew loud as the dream came back to him.

"There, there. Don't think about the ugly old dream. Think about nice, sweet things."

"But Mommy, he was—"

"Shhh," Julie said quietly. "No more about the dream. Let me sing to you."

Noah pulled his monkey tight to him and turned over. The song had a magical quality, chasing away badness, and pain, and fear. And though he wasn't sung to very often anymore, it still had a special power.

"Hush little baby, don't say a word. . . . Mama's going to buy you a mocking bird. . . ."

By the time Julie was singing that he was still the "sweetest little baby in town," she could see the steady rise and fall of Noah's chest as sleep reclaimed him.

She came back to the bedroom and saw that Jack had turned on his glaring Tensor lamp at his bedside. Their lovemaking, she surmised, was over and soon he'd reach for the hefty volume of Harlan Ellison's rantings and ravings that lay on his night table.

"Is he okay?" Jack asked.

Julie slipped back into bed, leaving her nightgown off. "Yeah. He was pretty frightened. Great sense of timing, huh?"

Jack smiled. And then the phone rang. "Jeepers. Busy night."

"Hello," he said, picking up the flimsy twenty-dollar phone. He glanced at the clock. 10:50 at night. Pretty damn late for anyone to . . .

"Oh, Tom. Hello." Julie listened, trying to imagine the other half of the conversation. "Right. Oh, Jesus. Whereabouts? Right. Okay. I will. Sure. No, no, it's okay. Thanks Tom." Jack hung up.

"Tom DeFalco," Jack said with a sigh. "It's about Helen Waverly." Julie nodded. She knew Helen only to see on the street. She was part of the neighborhood, like the fat old oak tree near the corner, or the playground next to the elementary school. Julie knew her smile, and the sense of strength that came from it. When Jack had told her that she was apparently missing Julie had thought that she had gone to a friend's house, that it was just a misunderstanding. She would certainly turn up.

But now she knew there was something wrong.

"They found a shoe, a brown woman's shoe. It was just lying near the curb. Somebody putting out their garbage found it."

"Oh, God," Julie said quietly. "Are they sure it's hers? Maybe someone threw it out with the trash, maybe a dog grabbed it, and pulled it down the block. . . ."

Jack shook his head. "They asked everyone on the block. No one identified it. . And no one said they heard anything. Maybe there was nothing to hear."

Here he paused, wondering what it all meant even as he told his wife. "They found it on Schuyler Road."

Three blocks, Julie thought. Just three short suburban blocks away. She reached down on the floor for her nightgown. She lay back, and turned away from Jack's light. She heard him pick up his book. And, except for the steady sound of him turning pages, all around her was quiet.

In the next room, the dream was trying to begin again in Noah's sleeping brain. But he pushed it away, telling himself that it was just not real.

But he never got to tell his Mommy, he thought. He never got to say that it wasn't her little Noah that the man was after. And by the morning he would have forgotten it all.

Two blocks away, Elliot Parks was sitting next to Vicky Sloan, inside his father's well-padded Chrysler LeBaron. Not exactly his choice of wheels, but it was roomy enough for what he had in mind.

And it had a terrific tape deck, now pumping out some garbage by Tears for Fears. Pure junk, he knew, A-Number-One trash, but dynamite make-out music. At least that's what he thought.

They were still at the talking stage. Elliot was going "deep," as he termed it, talking about what he wanted to do with his life and where he was headed. As captain of the swim team, he knew he had the physical side of things covered, but a girl like Vicky—smart, blonde, and loaded—was looking for a lot more. She would want a bit of soul and a lot of ambition. So Elliot was ready to portray the athlete-cum-poet. Dylan Thomas in skin-tight briefs.

Whatever it would take to get into her pants.

As far as Elliot knew no one at Harley High had opened her golden portals yet. While not exactly a cock teaser, Vicky had a lot of guys stirred up with no hope of success. But Elliot wasn't in a rush. Just like in his strategy for the 100-meter free style, Elliot was ready to go the distance. All the groundwork was done, the dates, the parties, the "deep" conversations, all leading to the moment when, with the right turn of a phrase and his wrist, the tumblers would fall in place and the gates to paradise would pop open.

And, man, she looked great tonight. She had on a short turquoise skirt and low-cut blouse, while her tan belonged in a Coppertone ad. Her eyes were on him as he spoke of "his future," and he knew he was halfway home.

But then she saw someone walking up the street.

"Elliot," Vicky said. "Who's that?"

Elliot was just able to make out a figure standing in the shadows. "There? Oh, I don't know. Probably just . . ."

"You know, maybe we shouldn't be out. That boy disappeared from near here. . . ."

"Hey, never fear. I'm here to protect you." Elliot

put his arm around Vicky and pulled her close. Current events weren't his forte, but he had heard his parents talking about the disappearance. But, as Mr. T might say, he pitied the poor fool who tried to mess with him. Pumping iron and six years of Tae Kwon Do had made him confident.

"Oh look, baby. It's just someone walking his dog. See?"

Vicky did see. Someone flopping around in his slippers and pajamas while his miniature poodle sniffed around for the ideal spot to "make." She laughed.

"Yeah," she said. "I guess I'm just jittery." A police car went by, slowing to look them over, then moving on. Vicky relaxed, leaning comfortably into Elliot's firm body.

"Sure. But I'm here. Master of the Ancient Arts of Self-Defense. Any problem and I'll kick ass." He paused here, wanting to get his seduction back on track. "Y'know, you're beautiful in this moonlight." He winced even as he said it. He leaned forward to kiss her small lips, imagining a spark coming from her. "I really care for you, Vicky. You mean a lot to me."

The kisses were returned. Not, he knew, with the full burst of heat he had gotten from his old flame Patti Berne, but returned nonetheless. Like a high-speed computer devoted to merely one task, Elliot's mind calculated the data from her responses even as it planned the next phase in his assault, constantly weighing the risk of rejection.

After more kisses, the big move, to her small, cone-shaped breasts, brought the first setback. "No, Elliot.

60

Please," she said quietly. He pulled back gently. "I mean, not so fast. I like you, I like you a lot. But give me some time."

He paused, staring right into her gleaming eyes. Sure, he thought. You, sweetheart, are worth the wait. Not forever, but for a while. I'll get there yet.

"Sure, Vicky. My feelings just pushed me a bit. Whoa! Look at the time. I promised your dad you'd be back by twelve. We'd better get going." He leaned over to give her a reassuring kiss.

He quickly resumed a light tone with Vicky, chatting about plans for a Jones Beach trek that weekend, making sure not to act put off. That could be deadly, he knew. He pulled up in front of her house, a bright porch light awaiting her return.

He hopped out, ran around to her side, and opened her door. She walked quickly to the porch, looking left and right, and he realized that she was really scared despite his martial-arts bullshit.

"Good night, Elliot," she said, turning quickly to him and giving him a kiss that was now warm, open, promising more to come. Elliot watched her enter the house and shut the door behind her. Then the porch light went out.

He walked back to the car. The half moon filled the street with a bluish light and a soft breeze cooled his bare arms. He got back into the LeSabre, ejected Tears for Fears, and popped in Frankie Goes to Hollywood.

"Relax," he sang with the band. "Don't do it. . . . When you gonna come . . ."

The music escaped through the open windows, and people still awake could hear Frankie clear as a bell. But, except for a single police car, Elliot saw that he was the only one about. Such a quiet, sleepy town, he thought. Summertime was Boredom City in Harley. If it wasn't for his clerking job at the Food Emporium and Vicky's sweet buns, he wished he could be almost anywhere else. Maybe Malibu, or Daytona Beach, or . . .

Shit. No light on his porch. That meant that his old man was pissed at him. His father was even stricter than most of his dates' parents. But it was the car Mr. Parks was concerned about. He imagined Elliot bringing home the steel-gray Chrysler looking like a veteran from a Mad Max movie. Elliot shut the tape off.

He eased the car into the driveway so, if his dad was listening, he'd hear the smooth way Elliot brought the car home. He stopped in front of the garage and fiddled around on the floor searching for the electric door-opener.

It was down there somewhere, he thought, as he groped under the bench seat. "Where the hell," he said aloud. And then he had it. He pointed it at the garage and pressed a button. The door-opener was a sleek, silent machine, designed not to awaken any neighbors.

He pulled the car in, nice and straight, leaving no doubt that it was parked by one sober buckaroo. Then he turned the ignition key and killed the lights. He stepped out of the car and slammed the door behind him.

He wasn't alone.

It was a feeling at first, a creepy notion that he was being watched. Then there was a small sound.

A tiny rustle.

A raccoon in the shadows perhaps, a mouse maybe, or some other rodent that had entered the garage in the wake of the car. Happened all the time in the winter. The cat loved it in here. In the winter.

There! Another rustle. The moonlight was glaring in Elliot's face, but the other side of the two-car garage was pitch black behind its closed door.

With a steady pace he walked out, losing all his bravado about pitying the "poor fool" who'd mess with him. He was just a little edgy from being with Vicky, he told himself. That's all. And, hell, it was dark in here.

He took four steps. Enough to see his split-level ranch home, the pool in the backyard, the driveway running down to the deadly quiet street. Four steps, and he knew he was in trouble.

Someone grabbed him. A hand covered his face (so damn big, he thought panicking—and tight, fitting like a mask over his mouth). Then an arm was around him, closing around his mid-section. Then, oh sweet Jesus, Elliot felt himself being lifted into the air.

He was a boy then, a little boy awakening in the middle of the night, crying out for Mommy and Daddy to please come and end this nightmare. Please send the bad man away, he'd ask through his tears. And they'd talk to him, soothe him, until the dream had evaporated leaving nothing behind. And he'd return to sleep.

But this was real, and he knew that he was on his own. He brought his elbow up sharply and, as he had practiced many times, jammed it back and up, a devastating blow to whoever was holding him. You fucker, Elliot thought, trying to use his fear to fight back. He heard his attacker gasp. The hand around Elliot's mouth slid off. Elliot screamed for help.

It echoed in the garage, but only a little sound escaped into the summer night. The hand crept back. Elliot tried the same blow with his other arm. But it was too late. His arms were pinned now by his own body held tightly against his attacker. My God, Elliot thought, how could anything be that strong!

As he was dragged out of the garage, Elliot saw his face. Such an ordinary, kindly-looking face. He'd seen the face before but he couldn't remember where. At the Emporium, on the street, in his dreams? The man looked at him, his eyes boring into Elliot's.

Elliot felt himself relax, lost in contemplating those eyes, falling headlong into them. Like a lifeless dummy, Elliot was dragged, his mind as blank as though he was just coming out of some heavy anesthesia. He didn't wonder whether anyone could see him. He didn't struggle. He barely noticed the house, and then the back door he was brought to. He didn't stop to wonder whether someone out there was watching and calling the police.

Which, in fact, no one was.

Only when he reached the bottom stair to the back door and entered the basement did Elliot feel his mind clear. It cleared and he saw more faces, people he knew. Sure, he had sold them their groceries. Nice folks. Oh, this is okay he thought, this is . . .

The door slammed shut, and another heavy metal door was bolted behind it. Elliot tried to talk but found he was mumbling, stuttering.

"I . . . I . . ." Then he noticed the dark, purple curtain in front of him. And a chair, facing it, a chair with straps, and belts, and . . .

In front of it a large red spot glistened. Elliot tried to back away.

"Good," one of the faces said. "Let's get on with it."

He was pushed into the chair. When he started to get up, he found that he couldn't, he couldn't do anything. Just like in a dream, he thought, when you try to run and you *just can't do it*.

He was crying now, moaning, as one of the people began to pull back the curtain. And everyone in the basement gathered close to the chair, close to Elliot, as the screaming began.

Chapter 5

The Harley Pool was a private club, established in 1957 to provide an Olympic-sized pool, tennis courts, a snack bar, and an attractive cocktail lounge for its members. And, though it was nowhere stated in its original charter (drawn up by a VP with Merrill Lynch), membership was "restricted." You needed three members to recommend you to the club, and the membership knew exactly who was and who wasn't wanted. Everyone knew this, and people who prided themselves on their support of the civil-rights movement had absolutely no compunction about joining the lily-white club.

It wasn't too long ago that it was also an all-Gentile club. If any Jews inquired about joining, they were given membership forms, with a smile, and encouraged to find three members to recommend them. Which, of course, they never could do.

But amidst all the hurly-burly of the Sixties, with most people trying to keep their draft-age sons at home, off drugs, and out of a commune, concerns about Jews became secondary, and the first Jewish family entered the club almost unnoticed by the

Old Guard.

Which history Peter Jaffe, President of the Harley Pool and sometime member of Congregation Beth-Israel, was not totally unaware of.

His daughter Shelly, like most of the kids in Harley, practically lived at the pool. Even when all the near teenagers were summoned home for a quick dinner of charcoburgers from the gas grill, or some cold cuts left over from last weekend's backyard bash, the kids of Harley ran to the phones to talk of the next day's festivities. What time you gettin' there? they'd ask each other. Are you bringing your box? Should I bring my tapes? Is Joey coming? Is Mary coming with him? And on and on, dissecting every little detail of what would turn out to be a day just like the one previous, a day hanging out by the pool, doing nothing, with only an occasional dip into the chilly blue pool itself.

A day just like this Thursday.

Shelly Jaffe had staked out the north corner of the pool, a "neat" location according to her friends because of the equal proximity of the snack bar and the diving board. She was lying down on a heavy towel her parents had picked up in Hawaii. On it some dark-skinned surfer was depicted riding a really big wave, arms akimbo, as exotic birds and gladiolas danced around his head. To most tastes it would be garish, but Shelly felt that it showed she'd actually been in Hawaii—not Aruba, or Barbados, but the island-state itself, clear across another ocean.

Totally awesome.

And she was also, as she never ceased reminding Sarah, who was only twelve. Having five months on

68

her best friend gave Shelly a whole world of sophistication and knowledge that Sarah could only dream about.

Or so she thought.

She sat up. To her left lay Patty Myers, eager to do just about anything Shelly or Sarah might suggest.

"Jesus," said Shelly, sitting up on her towel. She checked that her bikini top hadn't slipped down. (There wasn't, she knew, a whole lot to hold it in place.) She was proud of her developing breasts but she was also more than a bit self-conscious. "Where the heck is Sarah Jane?"

Patty, sporting a more expansive two-piece suit, sat up, scanning the nearly empty pool, glancing at the exit door from the girls' lockers.

"It's still early."

Shelly nodded. "Look, S.J. said ten sharp, and it's half past. I hope the Harley Ripper didn't get her." She laughed.

"Wait. There she is. Coming in now."

"Oh yeah." Shelly waved at Sarah, as though Sarah might not know the spot Shelly had picked. Sarah lugged a large straw bag which had her towel, tapes, and a ham sandwich that would remain uneaten before joining the day's garbage. Day after day, Sarah and her friends existed on greasy french fries and Diet Cokes, while their mothers fantasized about nutritious lunches with cheese, milk, and fruit.

"Hey, girl. Where've you been? I thought we set the time for ten o'clock."

Sarah plopped her stuff down and unrolled a plush sea-green towel. "I know, but my mom's worried because of that Burdick kid and Mrs. Waverly."

"Mrs. Who?" Shelly asked.

"Mrs. Waverly. She lived near us and disappeared the other night. So my mom wanted to drive me over. I had to wait for her."

"Hi, Sarah," said Patty, who had been looking for a moment to squeeze herself in.

And Sarah, as if seeing Patty materialize before her eyes, said, "Oh, hi."

Silence fell while Sarah organized her stuff, and prepared to lie down. She took her tapes out of her bag, then her lotion, then her hairbrush, and finally a book—*Tiger Eyes* by Judy Blume. She picked up her hairbrush and brushed her long brown hair twenty sweeping strokes, caring little about the damage the sun and chlorine were wreaking on her normally lustrous locks. Her mother had suggested a sun hat, but Sarah sort of liked the frizzed-out look she was developing.

"She's picking you up too?" asked Shelly. She longed to have hair like Sarah's, annoyed at her own tight red curls.

"Yeah. All week I guess. Until they catch him."

"Why 'him'?" asked Patty quietly. "Could just as easily be a 'her.'"

"Doubtful, Patty-Cake," said Shelly. "I heard my dad tell my mom that the police know it's a guy, or something like that."

Patty retreated, just as a puffy cloud eased over the sun, sending the temperature down a few degrees.

"Well," announced Sarah, standing up, "I'm going in." She walked to the pool edge, knowing that they'd follow. I'm the real leader, she thought with a private smile. Shelly's got a lot of money, and Patty's easily ten times smarter, but they go where I go.

She dove off the edge, her body forming a graceful curve as it sliced through the air and into the water. Then she felt the cold water, so damn cold she thought, as if they somehow cooled the water, refrigerated it each night. And it only rarely got hot enough out to really enjoy the coolness.

She popped up, waiting for Patty and Shelly to surface near her. Almost in tandem they broke the surface laughing, smiling. . . .

Suddenly it was happening again.

Everything seemed to slow down. And the sounds in the pool became muffled. Sarah was looking at Shelly, at her smile, but she saw something else.

Shelly was crying, her head resting on the Jaffes' white enamel kitchen table, sobbing while near her stood two people. Her parents. And they were saying things to each other—no, not saying, *screaming*, screaming horrible things. Threats. Curses. While all the time Shelly moaned, begging them to stop, please stop. But they ignored her, and went on. . . .

And then it was gone.

The sounds of the pool resumed—the water lapping at her neck, the kids squealing as they came down the water slide, Shelly talking to her.

"Hey, S.J., what gives? We lost you there a minute. What's the matter? Forget that it's your period or something?" She giggled.

"G-ross," said Patty.

"Happened to me once," Shelly said.

Sarah tried to hide her disturbance, this strange

71

disorientation that filled her just as it filled her each time "it" happened. She dove under the water, seeking the silence, giving herself time to think. What is this thing? she asked herself. What is it she sometimes sees when she looks into people's faces? Fantasies . . . dreams . . . the past . . . the future?

But it always faded quickly, like a malicious thought that you hold for a minute, then begrudgingly let go. She swam to the side of the pool, and sleekly pulled herself out of the water.

"Some swim," Shelly said coming up behind her, gasping.

"I just wanted to get wet. Now if that fat old cloud would move away, I could warm up."

Shelly wrapped her towel around herself and crouched by Sarah's blanket. "What tapes did you bring?" she asked digging through Sarah's stuff. "Ah, good. ZZ Top. The Hooters. My man Bruce. Hey, where's David Lee Roth?"

"Not there? I must have left it in my tape recorder." Sarah tried to sound normal as the strange feeling faded.

"I'm just a gigolo, and everywhere I go, people say that I'm just foolin'," Shelly sang with an otherworldly baritone, provoking a laugh in Sarah. "Well, don't forget it for the party this Saturday. My dad's going to set up his tape recorder. You're coming, aren't you?"

"Yeah. I think so."

"Me too," said Patty, though she wasn't too sure anyone was listening.

"At least," Sarah went on, "they haven't said no. I

don't know about the sleep-over, though. My mom's going to call your mom later on."

"Then we're home free, S.J. Absolutely. My mom will sell the whole deal to your parents, I mean totally. Oh, this is going to be excellent. Hey, don't you think they'd like to get you out of the house for a night? They'll probably try shipping off bratty little Noah to one of your old Aunt Windbags."

A moment later the sun was freed from the cloud. The increase in heat was instantaneous, and the three girls, on cue, reached for their sunglasses and reclined on their towels.

"Tanning time," Shelly announced.

The conversation faded as they gave themselves over to the soothing sun. And only when another cloud happened to cross would they move on to another activity, to hit the snack bar, or stroll around the pool, or dive again into the chilly water.

After dropping off Sarah, and making sure that she safely entered the pool area, Julie took a protesting Noah to Mrs. Calvin's. Edwina Calvin was Julie's regular Thursday sitter, a pleasant, dependable woman who watched Noah every Thursday till three, letting Julie work.

Of course Noah let it be known that he'd rather be at the pool.

"It's not fair," he said pouting. Then, with added vehemence, *"You're* not fair. Sarah gets to have fun. I got to go with dumb Mrs.—"

"Noah," Julie said quietly. Mrs. Calvin is sweet,

thought Julie, even if she doesn't offer much in the excitement department.

By the time they got to Mrs. Calvin's house, Noah seemed to have forgotten the pool and was looking forward to chunky oatmeal cookies. After a quick peck on his mother's cheek, he scrambled out of the car. Julie watched Mrs. Calvin open the screen door for him.

She drove home quickly, eager to savor every moment of freedom. Time without kids moved much faster, she noted to herself smiling. A day can be dragging by, but give me a few hours of free time and it passes like minutes.

Julie pulled quickly into her driveway and parked the car. Her agenda was fixed in her mind, and she reviewed it as she made her way to the side door and the basement steps.

There were a couple of pieces she wanted to reglaze, big, oddly shaped planters that she wanted to layer with a rich swirl of iridescent reds and browns. She was tired of making them but they sold well.

Then there were other things she was working on, a set of narrow-stemmed goblets that might just be the most technically perfect pieces that she'd done. And there was no way she could ever charge enough to make it worth the time that she invested in them.

She was going downstairs now, reaching up to pull the light on above the steps. The basement was cool and dark, a pleasant place on a hotter day. But now it only raised goose flesh on her bare arms.

In the far corner of the basement was her workshop. A series of shelves held her works in progress, works nearly done and pieces more than likely to be abandoned forever. Her wheel, not used much, was off in a corner, while a big table for cutting slabs of clay stood in the center of the floor. Above it were two large extension lamps that could be pulled down wherever she wanted light.

She turned them on.

A clock radio, discarded from the bedroom nearly ten years ago, displayed the passing minutes.

She dug out a brick-sized piece of brown clay and placed it on the table. She looked at it, gauging the size of the piece she might need, and picked it up to slice it in half. There were sounds. Her breathing. The soft oozing sound as the clay was cleaved. And then, just faintly, the creaking of the top step leading down to the basement.

Julie held her breath. She heard another step and, in the shadows, could make out feet stepping down.

Should she call out? she asked herself. Should she say, "Who is it?" and let the meter man, prowler, or whatever know that she was down here? Or did he know that already? Back and forth she debated, as the man stepped down, into the light, and rendered the whole mental dialogue pointless.

"Hi, Julie. Thought you'd be here." The man stepped confidently into the light, his smile warm.

"Patrick. You shouldn't . . ."

"I know." He put his hands up. "I shouldn't be here. It is Thursday, though, right? Noah's over with Mrs. Whoever, Sarah's gone. . . ."

She looked at him. Patrick Caldwell, the man who

ran the Hudson Gallery and sold her pottery. The man who sold nearly everything she made. The man who made her life unhappy.

Julie stood up, trying to relieve her feeling of weakness. "Look, we said it was over. We agreed. . . ."

He smiled again, amused. "You said. *You* agreed. I never saw any reason to end anything." He stepped closer to her, and she didn't step away.

"No, Patrick. It's not good for me. I have my family, my kids. Damn it, I just can't go have a fling 'cause I'm feeling a little bored, a little tied down."

"Oh," Patrick said. "But it's not just that, is it? I mean, that's not all it is?" And he put his hand to her face, stroking it. "Is it?"

And she knew she should pull away, back up, and tell him to go upstairs, leaving no doubt about what she wanted.

But she didn't.

His hand stroked her, and all of a sudden the clay on the table didn't matter anymore. And all her resolve, her late-night promises to herself, meant nothing, fading in the shadows and light of the basement. Without her knowing it, she closed her eyes.

He kissed her, covering her mouth, her neck, and her mouth again with kisses that spoke of another life, other places—a world beyond He-Man at 4 p.m. and pre-adolescent trauma. It didn't matter. Not Jack, not the kids, none of it.

Patrick moved with experienced ease, giving no recognition of his victory other than moving with calm assurance. His hands moved under her shirt, searching, caressing, freeing her breasts even as he pressed against her, covering her mouth with his.

A single tear appeared in Julie's right eye. She moaned.

And outside the sun climbed higher, growing hotter as the hint of a haze began to appear in the early afternoon.

Chapter 6

"It's just a few yards ahead, Baker. There. See? Where the tall grass just disappears." Brian Mulcahy looked away from where he was pointing, looking instead at the tall black man by his side. His replacement, Mulcahy thought. Just one more month and it's goodbye to the Parks Department, goodbye to Westchester, and goodbye to the goddamn aqueduct.

"Yeah. I see it. How do you find it in the winter?" James Baker spoke with the earnest interest of a new employee. It was enough to make Mulcahy puke.

They both walked up the narrow path to the open area and looked down at the heavy iron grating before them.

"You look for landmarks. See that smokestack there, and the corner of that fence?" He watched Baker look back and forth trying to get his bearings. "Don't worry. You do this run enough times in summer and you'll know where all the ventilation shafts are. Hell," Mulcahy said laughing, putting a beefy arm around Baker, "you'll be able to find the fuckin' holes in your sleep."

But Baker just nodded, and Mulcahy awkwardly removed his arm. We'll never be drinking buddies, he thought. He resumed his role of teacher.

"Yeah. Every third ventilator from the aqueduct's got a ladder leading down." Mulcahy opened an old, over-sized canvas bag and dug out a large lug wrench. He fastened it on one of the four bolts holding the grating down. He turned it and, with a surprising lack of resistance, began screwing it off.

"Hell. I must've taken it easy screwin' this one in."

Baker looked on, not surprised by anything that the boobish Mulcahy could do. He wondered whether Mulcahy really hauled his fat ass down the tunnel as often as he was supposed to.

"There," Mulcahy said as the last bolt came off. "You know why these gratings are round?" Baker shook his head. "So's they don't fall in on a guy. They fit in flush. Here," he said as he lifted the heavy grating off the opening. "Put it on the grass . . . over there."

Baker received the grate with a groan. It was cast iron, damned heavy, and Mulcahy handled it like it was a piece of cardboard.

"Kids ever break in?" Baker asked Mulcahy who was already shining his sixteen-volt flashlight down the now-open tube.

"Nah. The bolts are too big, too hard to get off. Except this one. Damned if I know why they came off so easy. Well, let's start the tour. It'll be a hell of a lot cooler once we're in the aqueduct. Cooler in summer and warmer in winter."

Mulcahy went down first, flashlight held firmly in one hand while easing himself down step by step. He

80

wore hip boots that made a teeth-grating, squeaking noise as he descended. Baker felt funny, goofy almost, in his shiny boots, as though they were entering the belly of a whale. But there was no way of knowing just how much drainage water could be in the tube.

"C'mon man. Let's get going," Mulcahy shouted up, and Baker scurried down and stepped into the dark world of the Old Croton Aqueduct.

"Welcome to your new home," Mulcahy said, demonstrating the tunnel's echo. "And to celebrate . . ." Mulcahy rooted around inside his canvas bag and dug out two bottles. "Some Stroh's to seal the changing of the guard." Mulcahy handed one to Baker, who could barely make out the bottle in the reflected glow of the flashlight off the aqueduct walls. Mulcahy unscrewed his bottle and took a gulp. "Good-fuckin'-bye to this hole," he said and then he belched.

Baker laughed despite his best efforts to stay serious.

"C'mon, man, drink up." Baker shook his head. "You've got to. My last time in the Harley section of the tunnel. C'mon. There ain't any supervisors out here, boy." Mulcahy caught himself. You don't say "boy." Not these days. But then he smiled as he saw Baker open the bottle. "Later we'll piss on the wall to make it official." Mulcahy laughed.

Baker smiled, and looked down the totally dark tunnel, pitch black except for the little pool of light they were standing in. "It's pretty damn dark," he said.

Mulcahy nodded. "Just wait till your light goes dead sometime. Then you'll know how dark it really

81

is. I've hauled my fat ass out of here more than once."

"How far down does it go?" Baker asked.

"From here? It's about twenty-four, twenty-five miles to New York. The whole tunnel is forty miles long, from the Croton Reservoir to Central Park. And built by my people, I'm proud to say. Thousands of dumb Irish micks who came to this country thinking that the streets were paved with gold. Instead they ended up laying brick inside a tunnel for seventy-five cents a day." Mulcahy rapped his bottle against the wall, and the brick gave off a clear ringing sound. "They used brick to make the water flow smoothly, right to New York reservoir. Of course, back then Manhattan still had farms on it. Now it just has animals."

Mulcahy let out another belch, and it echoed through the tunnel. "We'd better get moving. I'm supposed to show you how to check the aqueduct tunnel, as if some day they might ever want to use it again. Damn waste of time . . ."

Mulcahy put his empty bottle into his bag. Baker chugged his beer down, and then hurried to put his empty in there also. Mulcahy started moving through the tunnel, a running commentary pouring from his mouth.

"You gotta check the ventilators. Make sure they're not clogged with plants, or garbage, or any kind of shit." They were both splashing briskly through the darkness. "You move your light back and forth making sure that there's nothin' and nobody down here. I only found one person down here, about ten years ago, just a little south of Tarrytown. The guy was in about five or six pieces. Someone rubbed him

82

out, broke in here, and hid the pieces. It would have been just as easy to . . ."

Baker saw Mulcahy stop short and point the light up to the top of the tunnel. "See that stuff?" Baker could make out odd brown tufts of what looked like fur, small roundish clumps that seemed fixed to the ceiling. "Don't worry about them. Just fur from the bats. But don't touch one. Could be it's a small bat all curled up." Mulcahy looked over and shined the light right in Baker's face. "Give you a real nasty nip."

He moved on, and Baker's nostrils were filled with the dank, somehow sickly smell of the tunnel. He saw strange patches of fungus growing on the bricks, just near where the drainage water lapped at the walls. Some twisted roots had made their way through a few of the ventilator shafts leading to the open air above, and they dangled like long bony fingers above them.

And there was no way, no way in hell that Baker could imagine doing this walk by himself, whistling in the dark, ducking the roots, moving under sleeping bats. No way. But maybe the beer and Mulcahy's bullshit just had him a little edgy.

They were due to come up about one and a half miles down the tunnel, just about on the outskirts of Harley. The hazy afternoon heat would be welcome after the coolness and the foul smells of the aqueduct.

Mulcahy stopped.

"What the . . ."

"What is it?" Baker asked. "What do—"

"Quiet." Mulcahy was aiming his light close to him, close to the tunnel sides near him. Then Baker saw something odd. It was some kind of netting. Yes, that's what it looked like . . . like a big fish net made out of some massive two-inch-thick rope. "Jesus," Mulcahy whispered. "It goes all the way down. All the way, as far as my light goes."

"Have you seen it before? Maybe something the Parks Department put in, or the Army Engineers? Maybe the bricks are starting to . . ."

But Mulcahy wasn't listening. He stepped closer to his left, shooting the light up and seeing that the netting did indeed go over their heads.

"It's like some kind of fuckin' trap. Like one of those damn lobster traps, you know?"

Baker nodded, though he had never seen a lobster trap in his life. He watched Mulcahy raise his left hand to the netting.

"I don't think that you should touch it, Mulcahy."

"It's weird. The strands have, like, pins or something coming out of them, fine little pins. . . ." His voice trailed off as he brought his hand close to the netting, gently, ready to just touch it, feather light, to see what it felt like.

"Hey, man," Baker started to say. But it was too late.

"Oh God," Mulcahy moaned, and he dropped the light. "Oh, Jesus. Help me. Oh, my god-damn hand. Grab the fuckin' light!"

Mulcahy moaned louder now, filling the silent tunnel with his bellowing. And behind him Baker thought he heard the flap of leathery wings.

Baker picked up the flashlight, which had landed just short of the small stream that ran through the defunct aqueduct. He moved next to Mulcahy, who was now crying out continuously.

84

Baker moved the light around. "What is it, Mulcahy? What happened?"

Mulcahy didn't answer, but he pointed to his hand to show Baker. It seemed stuck to the netting and Mulcahy seemed unable to pull it away. Several small, bloody rivulets were running down his arm.

"You've got to pull your hand away," Baker shouted, trying to be louder than the moans. "Pull it!" But Mulcahy was lost to his pain, holding his body away from the netting, writhing. Baker used the light to look at the needles protruding from the rope. Each one ended in a tiny hook, Baker noticed. Just like those burrs that grab at your socks and pants legs when you run through a thick, grassy meadow.

"Oh, God, Baker. Do something!"

And, not knowing whether it was right or not, Baker grabbed Mulcahy's massive arm and yanked it down, praying that the needles stayed in the netting and that Mulcahy's hand would come loose.

Mulcahy screamed but his hand came free, filled with dozens of bloody pockmarks.

"We've got to get you to the hospital, Mulcahy."

Mulcahy looked at the netting. "What is this shit?" he screamed. "If the Department put it here without telling me, I'm going to kick someone's ass."

"Yeah, yeah. C'mon, we'll go back to the shaft we came in by. I'll get you to an emergency room and tomorrow you can raise hell. I might even take you for a few beers."

Baker smiled. He reached down and picked up Mulcahy's canvas bag. "Hey, man, this is heavy." And he guided Mulcahy out, while the older man held his bleeding hand close to his stomach. The pain was ebbing, but Mulcahy's eyes teared in the darkness, glistening in the tunnel as they walked back to the stone ventilator.

Neither of them looked back, down the long aqueduct tunnel that led to the teeming millions who lived in New York City.

On Thursday night it always seemed as if people got some last-minute urge to buy a book, Jack Reilly thought. On Thursday, he kept the store open until 7:45, and the last fifteen minutes were always filled with frantic purchases. He looked at his watch. In five minutes it would be closing time. He'd lock the door and hustle the last few languid browsers out of the store.

"No, sir, the new Ludlum is not out," he said to the portly customer who had just asked him about the book. "It's not due till August."

The man cleared his throat. "But it was advertised," he said petulantly. "In the *Times*. I'm sure some other store must have it."

"No sir, I'm afraid . . ." But Jack found himself talking to a whispery, thin woman who had been hiding in the shadow of the now-departed thriller fan. He checked his watch again. Normally he'd be more relaxed about time. What's five minutes one way or the other? But tonight there was a Town Board meeting, an open work session due to start in fifteen minutes.

He took the young woman's money for the latest P.D. James mystery and, with a relieved smile, ran to the front door. His assistant, Emily, had one more customer but Jack announced to the remaining hopeful readers that the show, for tonight, was over.

As Jack turned the key in the heavy dead bolt, Emily was already shutting off the store's outside lights.

"Quickly, my dear. Affairs of State await me," Jack called to her. He walked over to the register and picked up a box labeled "reserves-filled." He rifled through a small stack of pink cards. He stopped at one.

"Emily, what's this? Some book ordered and picked up without a name?"

"Yes," she shouted from the sunken card-and-gift area just behind the register. "The man would leave only a number. Paid in advance, so I figured it was okay."

Now Jack knew that when some of his customers had a taste for exotic, erotic literature—normal-looking folk who had developed a liking for lurid tales of leather, whips, and worse—they were understandably reluctant to leave their names.

But this one was different. Jack read the card aloud.

"New York Underground, 1841-1941. What kind of book was it?" Jack asked as Emily came up to the checkout counter and grabbed her pocketbook. They started for the door together.

"Some kind of history. It's an old book. I was able to find it listed as a Greenleaf reprint, in their Civil Engineering section."

Jack turned the key on the door and pulled it open, and he and Emily entered the balmy summer night air.

"Ah, heat," she sighed, reminding Jack of her discomfort in the overly air-conditioned store.

Jack smiled. "Good night, Emily. See you in the a.m. And you can set the A.C. a couple degrees warmer."

Jack ran to his car, a battleship-gray Toyota whose insides resembled the padded cell occupied by a lunatic gorilla plied with Big Macs and Star Wars toys. Things, Jack was sure, lived under the bizarre pile of garbage that hid his car floor from prying eyes.

He pulled out quickly, eager to get to the board meeting.

He arrived in the small oaken chamber, the 100-year old Town Hall, just as the large Regulator clock clicked the arrival of 8 o'clock. And he saw something that he'd never seen since becoming mayor more than three years ago.

The room was packed. People filled the nine rows of pew-like seats, and standees lined the outer walls. Smoke filled the air, though a trio of signs warned that smoking was strictly prohibited and punishable by law. The board, sitting before a table on a small raised area in front, looked decidedly ill at ease. As soon as Board President Alice Payne saw Jack, she rapped her gavel and asked for quiet. Jack elbowed his way to the table.

"As you know," Alice Payne said, and then realizing that it was still far too noisy to go on, she rapped again. "Please!" And the hubbub, an angry sound Jack realized as he plowed through it, subsided slightly. "Thank you. As you know, this is an open board meeting, a work session. At appropriate times you will be able to comment on the items being discussed—"

Someone in the room snorted.

"Or ask questions. Please keep to the item currently being discussed. At the end of the work session, general questions and comments can be entertained." Alice Payne gave Jack a fearful glance as he slid into the end seat. Next to him was Henry Artsdalen, owner of Artsdalen Hardware, who sat silently through most meetings. Next to him was Pauline Niles, the mad budget-slasher of the group, and then Franklin Palmer, who used the board as a lifeline to new insurance sales. Jack knew Palmer to be a real vampire. There was a story that he once tried to sell insurance to a bereaved family at a wake. He was a member in good standing of the Million-Dollar Club and an A-Number-One, card-carrying asshole.

Jack noticed that Town Manager Bill Sloan was missing. Looking back now at the crowd, Jack knew that something ugly was up.

"The first item to be discussed is the—"

"Where's DeFalco?" The voice was low, deep, and rumbling from the back of the room. Payne tried to ignore it.

"Is the proposed development for—"

"Where's DeFalco?" And now the voice seemed even more powerful and the crowd turned to look at the man. Payne stumbled on her words, and then Jack saw her pick up the gavel. But it was too late.

"Yeah!" different voices from the crowd called. "Where's the Chief? Where is he? Where's he hiding?"

Alice Payne banged the gavel repeatedly, but to no avail. Jack looked around. Tom DeFalco usually did attend the meetings, though he rarely said anything unless directly called on by one of the board members. Where was he? Jack wondered.

"Where is the good Chief of Police?" the deep voice asked again, and Jack saw the man, moving slowly to the front, all eyes glued to him. The gavel seemed to wilt in Payne's hand. "How many more people have to disappear in this damn town before he gets his Keystone Kops police department doing something?"

The crowd yelled out their support.

The man was big, Jack saw. A short-sleeved shirt revealed the chunky arms of someone who was used to lugging heavy stuff around. But his bright blue eyes showed that there was an equally strong intelligence at work.

"Excuse me, I don't think . . ." Payne started in a whisper that faded to nothingness.

"Tommy Burdick. Gone." The man spoke, and the crowd, a mix of worried middle-class faces as well as rough ones snarling in anger, nodded its approval. Fear's alive here, thought Jack. You could feel it inside the room, mixing with the smoke and the sweat.

"Helen Waverly. Gone. Gone, except for a shoe left in the street." The crowd rumbled on cue, and the man finally reached the table, dwarfing it and the bedraggled board that sat before it. "And last night," he said slowly, stepping up to the platform, "last night my own son vanished."

Jesus, thought Jack, it's Elliot Parks's father.

"Where's DeFalco!" he yelled.

Alice Payne seemed on the verge of tears. Jack stood up quickly. "I'm sure he's working on it right now, Mr. Parks. I'm sure that everything—"

"You are sure of shit!" a high-pitched voice hollered from the rear.

Jack heard the sea of voices direct their anger at him now, an anger created by fear. And for the first time Jack felt that things here could get out of hand. Yeah, he thought. Someone's going to stand up and say, "Lynch 'em." And someone else will say, "I've got some rope." Bad Day at Black Rock . . .

"Did I hear my name?" DeFalco entered from the rear and moved quickly through the crowd.

"Yes, Tom," Alice said slowly. "Everyone here's upset about . . . they want to know . . ."

Parks turned to the Chief. "We want to know what the hell you're doing to find our people."

DeFalco looked around, ignoring the glaring eyes of Vinnie Parks. He saw his neighbors, people that he said hi to as he passed them on the street. He saw couples that he'd saved from cracking each other's skulls open. He saw Tommy Burdick's father leaning drunkenly against the rear wall. He saw the town, gone sick and scared because something ugly was afoot.

"Tonight," he said filling the room with his voice, "a special investigator arrives from Albany. He's an expert in dealing with missing, abducted, kidnaped children, as well as adults. We'll have a State Police detective team coming tomorrow morning. Every regular cop in this town," and now he turned to face Parks, "*every* copy in this town is working tonight, driving through the streets of Harley. And the best way you people can help them is to *go home*, get off the roads. It will make their job a damn sight easier."

It became quiet, and in the back some people started to slip away.

"Can we help 'em, Tom?" a voice called out. "Patrol the streets, maybe?"

"No," he said strongly. "No vigilante stuff. That will only make things worse. *Just go home*, and let us do our work."

Parks held his ground for a moment, and then, letting his pain recapture him, he stepped back. Without a word he turned toward the rear, joining the departing crowd.

"The stoning's over for tonight," Franklin Palmer said quietly. No one on the board seemed to hear.

"I think," Alice Payne said to the board members, "that we'd best postpone our agenda until next week. That is, if you agree." Jack could see that she was obviously shaken. Her training as a real-estate broker hadn't prepared her to quell a small-town riot.

"Good idea," Jack said. "I'd rather be home with my family."

"And I'd rather catch the Yankee game," said Artsdalen.

They moved uneasily, not wanting to seem to be rushing to the exit. Over our heads, thought Jack, that's what we were tonight. Panic is no toy for amateurs to play with.

He noticed DeFalco waiting around, watching the others move to the stairs.

"Jack," he said.

"No news?" Jack asked.

DeFalco shook his head. "Jack, do you got to run?"

92

"Well, I . . ."

"There's someone I want you to meet."

Jack gave DeFalco a strange look. "Who?"

"Captain Leander Merrit, State Police. The expert's here, Jack, back at the station. And the one person he wants to meet, my friend, is you."

Chapter 7

DeFalco led Jack Reilly past the front desk of the police station, past a crumpled drunk mumbling to the floor, to the row of offices at the back of the building. He opened a door to a small room ("For interrogations and pizza binges," he had once said), and told Jack to take a seat. In a minute he was back with Captain Merrit.

Merrit entered the room quickly. He was a large man, well-stuffed, Jack thought. But he also looked powerful. He had a thick head of dark curly hair and a flashy mustache. He seemed cramped in the room.

"Don't get up," he said to Jack. "Let me tell you why I asked you here. I need a guide, someone who knows Harley. Chief DeFalco says that, short of himself, you'd be the best man. Will you help me out?"

"Sure. Whatever you need. But I . . ."

"Good, good," Merrit said patting Jack's shoulder. "Tomorrow, nine a.m. sharp. I'll pick you up. First we'll hit the river. I have a diving team coming up to check the river for bodies. Then you'll teach me Harley. The neighborhoods, the parks, the hidden places. What do you say?"

Jack looked over to DeFalco, then at Merrit, who was obviously used to moving fast.

"Okay, but I run a store."

"Get someone in. For a few days. Oh, I'll need you for a night or two. Any problem?"

"My wife gets a bit jittery when I'm out. I'd rather . . ."

"Ask her if she wants to be able to take a walk again. Ask her if she wants your kids to play outside. And then ask yourself, Mr. Mayor, just whose town this is."

Merrit tapped a cigarette out from a deep red case, and Jack could read the name Rothman's. He lit the cigarette, not seeming to care that he had made Jack Reilly mad. He looked at him carefully.

"I've got to go, Jack. There's some pretty sloppy police reports I've got to read. No offense, Tom. Any questions that you'd like to ask?"

Yeah, thought Reilly. Where the fuck did you learn how to steamroller people? Instead, he said, "Just one. What do you think's going on?"

"Jack," DeFalco started to say, "I don't think the Captain should . . ."

Merrit raised his hand. "In America? The country's going to hell in a handcart, Jack. But here, in Harley? Well, what I say goes no further, got it?"

Jack nodded.

Merrit drew a big breath. "It's not a sex offender. They're age and type specific. Young girls, or old ladies, blonds, brunettes. And it's not a serial murder. No pattern. No kidnaping for money, that's pretty damn clear. So, what's left?"

"I don't know."

Merrit stepped closer to Jack. "Well, my friend, nor the fuck do I. Harley's got something brand new, off the books. A real record-breaker, Jack. Whatever it is, you poor bastards got it first. And you don't have a single damn clue worth the name."

Tom DeFalco sighed, and Merrit turned to him.

"Easy, Chief. Our boy here can stand the truth. And now, gentlemen, I have my reading to do."

Merrit walked out the door. Jack got up to follow him out. DeFalco grabbed his arm.

"Thanks, Jack. You could have said no."

"Could I?" Jack laughed. And then, as he walked out of the station, a strange image came to him. It was another mayor, a little three-foot high fellow dressed in a long green frock coat with a creamy-tan top hat.

The Mayor of Munchkin Land, he remembered. Standing before the corpse of the Wicked Witch of the East, pronouncing her to be "most sin-cerely dead."

"Right," he said aloud to the balmy summer night air. Well, there's trouble in this Munchkin Land and the Wicked Witch, whoever it is, is not yet dead.

Jack drove home slowly, fatigue washing over him, and the many tunes of Oz rang in his head.

Jack tried to make as little noise as he came in the front door. He shut the porch light off and kicked off his shoes. Then he looked up to see Julie standing halfway down the stairs, her hair tousled and her eyes blinking in the living room light.

"Asleep already?" Jack asked. It seemed as if lately

97

their sleeping hours had grown even more out of sync.

Julie nodded. "Noah's sick. Could you dig out the humidifier from the basement?"

"What's wrong?" Jack asked.

"He was sniffly this morning, but by the time he got back from Mrs. Calvin's it had gone to his chest. He's got a slight fever. . . ."

"Why don't you call Dr. Read?"

"I did. He said it's a summer flu. It's going around. I'm going to bring him in the morning."

"Okay. I'll go get the humidifier."

Jack walked back to the kitchen, to the steps leading down to the basement.

It was cool down here, Jack thought, seemingly a constant temperature in winter or summer. He walked over to the extension lamp near Julie's workshop. He needed that on to see the humidifier box on a nearby shelf. He switched it on.

The corner of the basement lit up and Jack saw the box, a respectable covering of dust on it. It had been a while since the kids had needed it. There was a time not too long ago when every month or two it was being used.

He reached up and pulled the box down, into the pool of light, onto Julie's work table. Then he saw something that made him pause. In the fine covering of dried clay on top of the desk were two clear handprints. He almost ignored them, and started to reach up to turn the light off.

But he stopped. The prints were clear, almost unsmudged in the powder. His heart was beating just a bit faster as he reached out to them, slowly, placing his own hands directly over them. And seeing . . .

Seeing that they were larger than his own hand. Something clicked behind him and he turned quickly. But it was just the hot water heater shutting off.

Jack turned the light off and carried the humidifier upstairs.

"Here we are," he said, entering their bedroom, but Julie wasn't there. A raspy, cackling cough was coming from Noah's room. Jack walked in.

"How's he doing?"

Julie held Noah tightly, patting his back. "He just woke up, coughing terribly. Can you set the humidifier up? I've got to take his temperature again."

Jack filled the humidifier with cold water while Julie laid Noah on his back. Always moving, on the go, never stopping till he got sick, she thought. And then he seemed so small, so frail, as if God was reminding her that everything we love, we can lose.

"It's okay, sweetie," she crooned. "You've just got a nasty cough."

"But . . . it . . . hurts, Mommy," Noah cried. "It hurts me."

Julie patted his cheek. "Here," she said sticking the thermometer in his mouth, "put this under your tongue. Daddy's setting up the humidifier so you'll be able to breathe more easily. Then I'll give you some cough syrup, okay?"

Noah, serious and silent with the thermometer held carefully in his mouth, nodded.

"Where shall I put this?" Jack asked.

"On the bureau. Aim the nozzle towards his bed."

She removed the thermometer. "One hundred and two. Still!" She reached over for a small container. "Here's some Tylenol, honey. They'll help your fever."

"Yuck!" Noah yelled, and Jack laughed. Noah took the medicine with a grimace worthy of a gargoyle.

In moments, Julie had Noah back in bed with the lights out. Except for the hum of the humidifier, his room was quiet.

"It's going to be a long night," Julie said tiredly, crawling back into bed with Jack.

"Yeah, I guess so," said Jack.

And Julie didn't ask about the town meeting, and Jack didn't tell her about it, or Merrit, or leaving her alone at night.

And he didn't ask her about the hand prints, and by the time he remembered, it just wouldn't matter.

Sarah stirred.

She heard voices, disembodied sounds that drifted in and out of her sleeping mind until she was awake. She heard the medicine cabinet open with a high-pitched squeak, and then Noah crying, his small voice erasing Sarah's normal distaste for her annoying little brother.

She heard her mother sing, and for a few moments Sarah remembered what it was like to be so small and protected, when a mother's song was enough to chase all the bad things away.

Sarah let her mother's barely heard crooning lull her back to sleep, back to her dream.

A special dream.

It was a wonderful dream, the type of dream that you hope you have over and over all your life. Filled with hidden meaning and adventure, the dream was a treasured secret for Sarah. Even in her sleep she was smiling as it started.

It's a hot sunny day, and the blue sky seems almost dark. The sun is glowing white hot and makes the sand almost impossible to walk on. But no matter. Sarah can run into the gentle surf, wet herself down, and then run back to the scintillating heat of the beach.

He's there, as he always is in this dream. Older than her, but not much. Just enough, she knows. Hair burned almost white from the sun, and a tanned, muscular body. And a cheerful, smiling face.

He's always in her beach dream, always there waiting for her, waiting for . . .

He darts away, again something that always happens, and Sarah follows, laughing, as he high-kicks into surf, turning to see if she follows. Sarah laughs, calls to him.

But he flashes his grin and darts away. Sarah eagerly follows him.

A wonderful dream, over and over, always the same, never . . . But then the boy runs away from the water, up toward the cliff-like dunes that gird the beach.

No, she wants to call. It's too hot to go running up there. We'll burn our feet. But the boy can't hear. The wind is blowing in Sarah's face and she realizes that her voice just can't carry. (In her bed, Sarah turns over, kicking her sheet off.)

The boy stops and waves at her, still grinning. He signals for her to follow.

So Sarah runs now, trying to ignore the burning sensation on the bottom of her feet as she steps on the sun-broiled sand. He's waiting for her, and she has to follow. Because that's the way it always is in this wonderful dream.

She gets close to him, almost next to him. She is sweating and panting.

Then she sees the tunnel. It's a big tunnel, large enough for both of them to walk into. And it's never been in the dream before.

But the boy seems to sense her confusion, and he smiles and says . . .

"Come in. It's cool inside."

He runs in, engulfed by the dark.

Sarah's feet are so hot now she must do something. Though she never has gone in the tunnel before, it must be okay. After all, the boy went in.

She follows him in, and immediately she is chilled. It's more than cool in here, it's cold. As soon as she's in, she wants to get out.

She looks for the boy. As her sun-streaked eyes adjust to the gloom, she can see him, leaning against the wall, close now.

Real close.

Her heart beats fast with a new excitement.

"Come over here," he says quietly, the golden streaks of his hair catching the light.

And she does.

A few steps away, that's all it is. And then the boy will be next to her.

She stands there, just a few feet away from him,

still smiling.

Something is on the ground.

Scurrying back and forth between his legs, nibbling on his toes, breaking the skin. Furry things with long tails, squeaking.

Rats.

Why doesn't he move? she wonders. Why doesn't he call out?

She sees the wall he's leaning against, glistening green with the slimy algae. But as she looks at the tunnel wall, she sees that it's moving too, tiny things squirming to break through the algae, small, pale worms popping through the slime and crawling onto his hand.

"Come here," he says grinning.

No, she shakes her head. His smile fades. Around his feet swarms of rats begin appearing, and the worms are crawling, caterpillar-like, up his arm.

Blisters appear on his face and chest, bulging and then popping open. He takes a step toward her.

She moves backwards, steps on something plump. A rat squeals out in anger.

The boy's face seems to age before her eyes, becoming a gnarled, twisted thing, grinning, leering at her. A worm-filled hand reaches out for her.

In a throaty, mocking voice the man pleads . . . "Come here, Sarah. I won't hurt you, honest I won't."

Sarah screams, and runs down the tunnel, runs as fast as she can, but the opening never gets any closer.

(Her hands dig into the mattress, and her toes work back and forth.)

She doesn't look back. She doesn't see the bent old

man shuffling after her, his hands still stretched out grasping, grasping.

She slips, and falls down in the slime. A mad party of rats come up to her face, nosing around, looking for a place to nibble.

Then the man is there, standing over her, reaching down for her. . . .

Her eyes opened. Quickly, with a desperate suddenness that brought her dark bedroom into focus. Noah was crying out again. Her body was covered with goose pimples, yet her bed sheets were damp from her sweat.

She heard her mother talking soothingly to Noah. Sarah lay there, listening, afraid to go back to sleep, afraid now to ever dream again.

It was the perfect house. A large porch circled around to the left before ending near the side entrance. White, unadorned pillars supported the second floor above it and provided pleasant leaning posts to watch a sudden summer thunderstorm or the first tentative snowflakes of a big snowfall.

The house had a sharp peaked roof, covering what was surely a finished attic, and two pairs of matched dormers, all sporting large windows veiled by curtains. The lawn was well cut, though not manicured, browning in spots now with the advance of summer. The front door looked to be a heavy piece of oak, with the black iron number 32 fastened to it.

It was a house where one could imagine rich Christmases spilling over with toys, cocoa, and festive family dinners. Or quiet evenings sipping a cold beer on the porch while the summer constellations came out. A house to live in, and fill with memories until it was time to pass it on to someone else.

And all of this was lost on Eddie Dixon, who saw only the size of it and imagined its hidden wealth. He looked for other things, like windows that could be easily opened with a pen knife, and the type of lock guarding the side door. A glance for the tell-tale wires and electronic sensors of a home security system. And then, perhaps, a look at the nearby houses. How close were they? Would they hear him breaking in? Could they hear someone screaming inside?

And the house, down a quiet side street and nicely spaced from its neighbors, passed all of Eddie's checks. It was, he thought, the perfect house.

Which was a good thing because all of a sudden Harley seemed like the setting for the annual police convention. Patrol cars were scooting up and down the nearby streets, stopping to look over Eddie as he made his way to Schuyler Road and the house. As it grew dark, even Eddie, who was no rocket scientist, realized that he'd soon be stopped and asked to explain just what he was up to.

And when he thought of that, Eddie instinctively felt his back pocket for his knife, a seven-inch Norwegian job that neatly folded in half, thin as a pack of gum.

Eddie liked knives, though not in the almost amorous way some of the freaks in the joint did. He respected the blade, taught himself how to use it so that one jab, one slash was enough. A tool of his profession, that's all. Still, it gave him a thrill to reach back there, and just . . .

Touch it.

He decided to hide in the backyard of the house. He had noticed the thick shrubs that clustered near the garage. Back there, it was dark already. And if anyone saw him he could say he was just cutting through, taking a little shortcut. Sure, if anyone saw him . . .

But he felt lucky tonight.

The pale twilight made him a grayish blur moving down the driveway. Lights were on in the house, but he knew, just knew, that no one would look out. His heart barely beat fast as he slipped behind the bushes and nestled close to the large garage. He sat there. Waiting. Dreaming.

He dreamt of jewels, silver, maybe even some cash—nice and smooth. He dreamt of tiptoeing upstairs to whatever sleeping farts lived in the house. And then waking them. Just a gentle nudge, letting them slowly blink to alertness but moving too quickly for them to make things messy. He dreamt of their eyes, wide open, with pupils big and dark in the shadows, and the wonderful-terrible way their mouths would fall open.

And maybe, if it went really smoothly, he'd stick around Harley and try to leave his mark on some other good citizens.

Eddie waited for the lights to go out. The sky went from deep blue to a hazy black flecked with stars. The lights stayed on, even when most of the nearby houses seemed completely dark. He started to consider doing the job with the lights on. Hell, everyone goes to bed once in a while and leaves the

106

lights on. Sure, they're probably asleep, or maybe even out somewhere. Maybe on a vacation.

So he talked to himself, inside his mind, dealing with the various possibilities and, to the best of his limited understanding, the possible outcomes. He stood up and moved toward the side door, his right hand slipping to his back pocket, feeling the knife, feeling strong.

Then, the lights went off. Downstairs first. A few minutes later the second floor went dark. Eddie stopped walking and stood there. Still could be a timer, he told himself. Or could be they just went to bed. With the curtains on the windows he couldn't see anything. He waited. Five minutes. Ten. He had no way of knowing how long he stood there. When he felt that they had to be asleep, he started again toward the side door.

It was like having no door at all. A single button lock that he had open in seconds and a thin chain that he pulled off the inside of the door with a smooth, almost soundless jerk.

He was in. He moved through the kitchen, feeling his way to the front of the house where he knew he'd find the stairs. Of course, he'd have to take care of the people first. Then he could take his time, look around leisurely, and see just what his prize was.

He found the stairs, his night-adjusted eyes picking out the small glints of reflected street light off the handrail and the wooden steps. He walked up silently, breathing shallowly. And as he moved he reached into his back pocket and pulled out his knife. He didn't flip it open in the way he so enjoyed doing, with a sharp, satisfying "click." No, one hand held it

107

while the other gently slipped the blade out slowly, until it was ready.

The top of the stairs confused him.

There were three, maybe four rooms. It was too dark to tell. Any one of them could have someone in it. He'd have to be real quiet, he told himself, and check each of them out before making a move. He moved left and saw two closed doors across from each other. Eddie opened the first, taking plenty of time, and he saw that it was some kind of storeroom, with crates and stacks of books filling the floor. He moved over to the second door. Again, he opened it gently, turning the knob silently.

There was a bed there, a single bed, empty and narrow just like those Eddie knew in prison. He could make out a mirror, a bureau, a closet. And nothing else.

He took a breath. The last room, then. He gripped his knife tighter, eager now to just end it and get on with searching the house. He wondered what time it was.

The third door was also shut. Eddie reached out and turned the knob as slowly as he was able. Then he pushed it open. The door creaked. Once, then again more loudly. Loud enough, surely, to wake up anyone. He entered quickly, jumping in, ready to strike.

The room was empty. Totally empty. The window was shut tight and, except for the curtains, there was no sign that anyone lived here. And Eddie, in his limited experience, had trouble identifying just what was starting to bother him.

There was nobody here, though. *That* he was

108

sure of.

So he searched the house, throwing the lights on in all the upstairs rooms, looking in the empty closets, dumping out empty bureau drawers, digging through crates filled with books that fell apart even as he handled them. And there were no jewels, no wallets bulging with cash, nothing. It was as if he had broken into a deserted house.

He went downstairs, growing more angry, digging his knife into the sofa just to cut up something. Everywhere he looked there was nothing of value. The kitchen contained a few plates, some cheap cutlery, a cup, a glass. A half-empty bottle of wine was on the table.

"Shit," Eddie Dixon said aloud.

He remembered, then, the attic and the basement, two places that he hadn't checked out yet.

"Probably nothin' there either," he muttered as he reached out for the bottle of wine, holding it up, finishing it. It was dry, bitter to his taste, but it felt good going down. Maybe, he thought trying to think the whole scene through, maybe if someone's moving out they're keeping their stuff in the attic. Or maybe in the basement.

It was close, the basement was. Right next to him.

He went over to the steps, passing an open metal door. He felt around for a light switch and, after jabbing his hand on some kind of hook, found it. He could see downstairs now and he went down, and then around to face a dark purple curtain.

Eddie's mind registered only a few things in those moments. His first thought, landing with a sickening thud in his gut, was that there was nothing down

It was red.

Yes—a burnt ochre where there should be blue. Geez, buddy, better get this fuckin' TV repaired because you've got some *major* problem with the color. And what the hell kind of bird is that? It's all . . .

Teeth. Snapping off the tendrils of the plants, darting away from the grasping leaves.

And so real, Eddie thought. Like I can touch it, just reach out and *fucking touch it*.

Don't touch it, Eddie's mind suggested. And he didn't. He backed up. He could feel his heart beating now, yes, and fast, the way it did the first night in jail, the night he screamed that he couldn't stand being caged. Yes, just like that. Not fear, no, he wasn't afraid. Not Eddie. But the knife seemed silly in his hand and he stepped back again.

One more look. Something coming now, near those trees. Something walking. Maybe he could watch it.

But Eddie turned away, knowing it was time to leave, to get out of here and go someplace where they play by the rules, with sleeping people and bulging wallets on the night table.

"Going someplace?" the man's voice said. He had simply appeared there, just behind Eddie.

"Right!" Eddie yelled. "Out of the way, fuck-face!" The man was tall, thin. An odd, angular man. Easy pickings if he tried to stop him, Eddie knew. He moved towards the steps.

He didn't move.

He looked down and saw that he hadn't moved an inch. He tried again. But nothing happened. He looked back at the mirror.

Something *was* coming, through the stick-like trees, through the clutching plants that cleared a path before it. Eddie could just make out a bit of color. It was a shiny, dirty gray, like ... like ...

Like one of those eels that fill the bottom of the Hudson. Sick-looking things that flop around in the sun trying to squirm their way off your hook and back into the muddy river bottom.

"Why can't I move?" Eddie screamed.

"Because I won't let you," the man said with a matter-of-fact smile. "I want you to stay. I've been waiting for you, you know, sipping wine, waiting. You see, you're the right one for tonight. You're just ..."

Perfect.

"Your fear is rising so quickly now, so fast. It's wonderful. But don't bother with me. Turn around. Turn around and look. Look!"

Eddie shook his head, but his feet shuffled slowly and he turned, finding himself saying the same thing in his mind over and over again.

Oh God. Oh sweet God. Let me go, please let me go.

He shuffled until he faced the mirror, faced the blackish-gray thing that came towards him. And he thought he heard a terrible banging around on the doors, on the walls, all around him. But it was just his heart pumping blood, squirting it madly through his system, trying to get him ready. His breath came in great gulping gasps now as he fought to breathe. And then he took a step toward the thing and he gave himself completely over to the horror.

PART II

Chapter 8

The Grand Canal.

And yes, thought Eli Singer, isn't it grand the way bits of garbage swirl in the polluted Venetian canals, chunks of lettuce, a wine cork, and, if you were really lucky, a dead rat?

How romantic to be in a gondola, a full moon above, reclining on garish red pillows, letting your hand slip down, outside the boat, to touch the water. Then, something brushes against your fingertips, something hard and spongy, with a tight, coarse pelt and a long, snaky tail.

Ah, Venice. And while I'm categorizing the wonders of the city of canals, thought Dr. Singer, let's not forget the smell of Venice. Surely it's much worse than the heavy, car-exhaust stench of New York, or the ripe odor of garlic, fish, and wet streets that fills a Parisian morning. Inhale deeply, and smell Venice, smell the open sewers, smell the dirty pathways where people urinate in the shadowy corners, then pray for a life-giving breeze from the Mediterranean.

Someone knocked and Eli Singer, sixty-one years old, moved slowly from the porch overlooking the

But you see, Singer thought, my heart has already given out. There's nothing there.

Nothing.

Except one thing, one simple, shining idea that would keep him from joining all the other old intellectuals who had chosen to die in Venice. Eli Singer knew that, if only his body would hold up, it was still important for him to be alive. In fact, he might even be the most important person in the world.

And at that, he allowed himself a sad smile. Again he checked a pocket, on the other side this time, digging out a large black billfold. His gnarled fingers slipped out his passport, and then the airplane ticket encased in a gaudy orange and blue envelope. He looked at the ticket.

Kennedy Airport. Arrival on Friday, at 4:30 p.m. E.D.T. One way.

There was another knock, and now Singer moved more quickly. It was arriving late, this strange crate from within the heart of the Soviet Union. Almost too late to matter. But still it was something he wanted to see, something he wanted to feel. To take the measure of it.

To touch the beast.

He opened the door to two burly deliverymen, both wearing a full sweat and morning bread crumbs. Deliveries in Venice were never easy, and the men here were unabashed about showing their great efforts.

The crate was about 60 by 100 centimeters, Eli could see, bigger than even he imagined. He reckoned it had cost him close to $5,000 just to get it smuggled out of the village of Tazovskoye. It was, quite simply, the first proof. The first physical proof of his odd little theories scorned by other anthropologists and archaeologists. And now it's here when it just doesn't matter anymore.

They lifted the crate up on one corner.

"Alt!" Singer said quickly. Then, "Gentile, signori." And he watched them slide the crate off the dolly onto the pale orange rug in the sitting room. The men went for their crowbars to open and Singer again cautioned, "Gentile."

First the top was popped off, exposing a thick burlap hiding the prize beneath. Then one of the men wedged the flat end of one of the bars into a corner crack, opening up one side of the crate. They grabbed for the burlap-covered object to pull it out onto the carpet.

Too rough, thought Singer, and he held up his hand to slow them. Now, with an awkward gentleness, they slid the prize out of the crate. One of the men, a large fellow with thick, hairy forearms, reached into his back pocket for a razor.

"Non," Singer said. And he dug out a few more 1,000-lire notes and gave them to the men. They smiled and nodded to the rich old man, not even curious about what they had struggled to unload in this grand suite in the Hotel Cipriani. They backed out, shutting the door behind them.

He was alone. Eli Singer had hoped that Mikhail could have been here. It had been his find, after all. But they had found him, probably cut his body into a dozen pieces, and threw them into the Black Sea. And the others? The few friends and former students were

120

scattered throughout the world, watching, waiting, ready to let Singer know that it was time.

Singer grabbed the long silver shears from the writing desk and began to cut the burlap, very gently, not wanting to damage the plaster beneath. He peeled it away, exposing wads of crumpled newspaper. He checked his watch. Fifteen minutes more and the taxi-boat would be here.

He hurried, working more quickly, pulling hard at the burlap, pushing the paper aside until, at last, it was exposed. And for the first time he felt the fear hit him in such an intense way that he almost turned from the object.

Imagine . . . he used to tell his students, imagine your worst nightmare. You know, the ones where it doesn't do any good to tell yourself that it's only a dream. And even waking up doesn't seem to help.

This was only a plaster cast, badly marred in spots by chipping and cracked in places. Parts of it were still coated in the vaseline-like gel used to make the cast.

But there was no mistaking the shape.

It looked like some kind of practical joke, a fake rigged up to trick the tourists, like the Piltdown Man, the giant found in the nineteenth century that was a fraud. But the northern woods of Siberia rarely had a call for tourists, and the print had been found in an almost totally deserted location.

It was a foot, if your imagination could stretch to call such a thing a foot. Found in the clay near the Tunguska River Basin, it looked more like some twisted appendage from a lobster's underside. There was a kind of oversized heel leading to an exaggerated

121

arch (perhaps capable of suction like a Ginko lizard) and it split into twin prongs, each curved and ending in a deep talon-like shape.

A foot, nearly seventy centimeters long.

And the rest? Oh, Singer could picture that. He had seen the old books with stylized drawings, and he had touched the faded carvings inside Mayan tombs, and he had held the strange wooden toys, like voodoo totems, found buried on the island of Roanoake.

Yes, he could imagine what had made that footprint.

The phone rang. He picked up the delicate receiver and heard the Direttore of the hotel announce the arrival of his taxi. At last the taxi was here, sputtering near the canal entrance to the hotel, spewing smoke into the air and iridescent trails of gasoline in the water.

Dr. Eli Singer grabbed his bag and made his way to the elevator and downstairs. He walked out to the small stone dock and looked to his right, toward the wonderful La Fenice Opera House, and then straight ahead, towards San Marco, and the birds, and the tourists, and the sea.

The last time, he thought sadly, overcoming his disgust with the city. It's always been hard to leave Venice. But this, the last time, would be the hardest.

He got into the big boat, and he tried to savor every moment of his leaving the dirty city.

Chapter 9

"How goes it, champ?" Jack sat down on the edge of Noah's bed. Dozens of Darth Vaders glared at him from the Star Wars sheets.

Noah, however, was curled up, kitten-like. His eyes were open, and he lay very still. "Okay," he said with no sincerity.

"No, not okay," said Jack. "Okay is when you bounce up and down on the bed doing squat thrusts and tucks. This is definitely not okay." Jack put his hand on Noah's warm head. "Would you like to lie on the couch downstairs and watch TV?" Noah made an almost imperceptible nod with his head.

"Okey-dokey," said Jack, scooping up his son. "You've got it."

He carried him down, thinking for a moment about the hundreds of times he had picked up Noah. And some day, he knew, he'd pick him up for the last time. And part of his life as a father would be over.

He placed Noah gently on the couch, arranging a fat pillow to cradle his head. Jack went to the TV and searched the channels.

"Scooby," Noah said quietly as Jack passed the

cartoon featuring a ghost-busting dog.

"Sure, guy. Anything else you want?" Noah didn't answer, giving himself over to the crash-bang world of the cartoon.

Jack went into the kitchen. He saw Julie dressed up, looking trim and exciting in a light summer dress. She even had heels on. Sarah was eating Cheerios and reading a book.

"I brought Noah down," he said. "He can watch TV. Good morning, sweetheart," Jack said to Sarah.

Julie went to the bathroom and started combing her hair. "He's still got a fever," she said. "When the poor baby gets sick, he gets really sick."

"Dad," Sarah said, her voice light with an exaggerated sweetness, "have you decided about the sleep-over?" She was already in her pool gear, an unchanging outfit of shorts, a Huey Lewis T-shirt, and sandals. Ah, Jack thought, to be young in summer, when the days just drift one into the other until one day you wake up and it's a chilly September morning.

But he turned to his wife instead. "Julie, why are you all dolled up?" There was the faintest hint of an edge of his voice.

Julie gave him a single glance and then returned to the mirror and her brush strokes. "I'm meeting some art buyers from a few New York galleries. One of them buys for the Museum of Modern Art's gift shop."

"But Noah . . ."

"I'll only be gone for an hour. Mrs. Calvin will be here to watch him."

"Dad," Sarah said, her voice taking on a more

purposeful tone. "What about—"

"You know Julie, I don't think it's such a good idea to run down to Caldwell's gallery when Noah is so sick."

"He's got the flu, Jack, the flu. My being here won't make it get better any faster."

"Yeah," Jack said raising his voice, "sure, but he just might like his mother nearby and not some old bag who—"

"Good, then you stay here. Christ, I've had this appointment for a month. I have my life too, my work, though you'd probably be a whole lot happier if I sat here watching game shows and making your mother's famous lasagna."

"Isn't that what you do anyhow?" Jack yelled.

"Well?" asked Sarah, her voice joining the melee. "Can I?"

Jack turned to her. "Can you what?"

"Can I sleep over after Shelly's pool party tomorrow?"

"No."

"Why?" Sarah bleated.

Jack looked at her. "Now now, Sarah. I don't want you out of the house overnight. Not now. Not till it's safe."

Sarah stood up, a major pout in the making, and she grabbed her Torchlight novel ("Where Romance Encounters Intrigue," the cover proclaimed) and marched out of the kitchen.

"I don't see why she can't go to the sleep-over," Julie announced matter-of-factly. "It's not like she'll be out on the street."

The phone rang just as Jack was about to explode

125

in anger.

Instead he picked up the receiver and said, "Hello? Oh, Emily, hi. No, don't worry about the deposits." Emily was sounding even more overwhelmed than usual. "I'll swing by and pick them up after lunch time. No, don't worry. You'll do fine. You run the store most of the time anyway. And I'll check in. Not to worry. Bye."

Jack snapped the phone down. Julie was putting on blush now, making one of her rare transformations into a bona-fide knockout. And all the trappings never failed to stir Jack, even when he was mad. Maybe, he thought, even more when he was mad.

"Shit," he muttered quietly.

He poured a cup of coffee and walked out to the living room.

Scooby-Doo had given way to She-Ra, Princess of Power, and Jack watched blankly, not comprehending the subtle machinations of Moss Man, Hordak, and the rest of the Evil Horde.

A horn beeped outside. Jack went to the window and saw Merrit sitting in an unmarked car. He came back to Noah, and whispered.

"Get better, champ. We need some energy around here."

He walked out to the Captain's car, a sleek black Chrysler with special New York State plates.

When Jack entered the car, a cloud of smoke greeted him. The atmosphere inside was like an arctic smog. Bracing cold from the air conditioner was laced with just enough carbon monoxide from cigarettes to send inexperienced lungs into a full-blown panic. Merrit said good morning while Jack coughed.

"I hope you don't mind if I smoke," Merrit said laconically. Then, without a pause, "Do I make a right to get to the river?"

"Yes. But why the river, Captain? I thought that you wanted to see the town."

"I have to meet some people first. Won't take long. Then we'll get on with the tour."

Jack waited. Then, when more information wasn't forthcoming, he asked, "What people?"

Merrit looked over and smiled, the smile of the pro initiating the amateur into their secret rites of missing bodies.

"Divers. There's a boat down there with a diving team from New York. They have a boat with some kind of sonar gizmo. It's a nifty little device that picks up stuff from the river bottom."

"Turn here," Jack said.

"Sure. Anyway, it gives a neat little picture of the bottom. Anything bigger than a beer can will show up. And if it looks promising, the divers go down and take a look."

"How pleasant."

"Look, Jack," Merrit said looking over at him. "Don't think I'm flippant. Stuff like this, in a small town, well, it can get pretty grim. But I can't go around wearing my concern on my sleeve. I have a job to do, and sometimes it gets grisly. Missing people sometimes equals missing bodies, and missing bodies have a knack for turning up in rivers, lakes, ponds, all sorts of places. You name it."

Jack nodded. And they drove in silence, past a quiet Main Street and down the hill to cross the train tracks. Jack looked out the window, then asked, "Are you meeting them at Alcott's Boat Yard?"

"I imagine so, if that's where one ties up boats. I just told them to get upriver to Harley and I'd meet them there."

"Well, there's the boat yard," Jack said.

"And there's the boat," Merrit said. He brought the car through the gate and drove to the end of the dock. He stopped the car and stepped out quickly. There were two divers moving gear around the boat, while someone else was hooking up wires to a large black console. Merrit reached over and shook hands with them, and then introduced Jack.

They were young, thought Jack, twenty-four, maybe twenty-five, but they seemed very serious, almost somber. The man at the console looked out of place, like some brainy assistant professor going fishing.

"They're really from Connecticut," Merrit said to Jack. "There's three teams the city uses, but this one's the best, aren't you guys? In real life, they help keep the peace in New Milford."

"It's choppy out there, Captain," the diver named Bill said. About as bad as Long Island Sound. How far do you want us to sweep?"

Merrit looked at Jack. "So what do you say, Jack? How far up or down before you're out of Harley?"

"You don't have to just look in Harley, do you?"

"No, but we'll start there. We can't search the whole river between Poughkeepsie and New York.

How far, then? Two miles? Three?"

Jack looked south, to the eastern end of the Tappan Zee Bridge, veiled in a faint morning haze. Eight miles to there, and another eight to the Bear Mountain Bridge. There's a lot of boats that use this part of the river. Fishing boats, sailboats, barges, tankers slogging up to Albany. Maybe even a boat dumping a little kid over the side.

"Four miles," he said.

The divers looked at each other, then Merrit. "We're not free tomorrow, Captain," the other diver, the shorter one named Tom, said.

Merrit looked up at the sky. "Then it's a damn good thing you've got a nice clear day. And I hear that you two do some of your best work at night." The divers laughed goodnaturedly at this, and Bill started to undo the lines holding the boat to the dock. "And call ship-to-shore as soon as you got something."

"Right, Captain," the man working the sonar said.

"C'mon, Jack," Merrit said getting back into his car. "Now you can show me Harley."

The Hudson was a strange river. The Atlantic Ocean rushed north nearly twenty miles to mingle with the fresh water from the Adirondack Mountains. By the time the headwaters from Lake Tear of the Clouds finally reached the harbor of New York City, they had already been caught many times in the steady ebb and flow of salty, brackish water that stretched from Manhattan to Harley. Harley was at

129

the breaking point; salt-water animals lived here, crabs, mussels, and eels that spawned in the floating plants of the Sargasso Sea. But freshwater fish could dart briefly into the slightly salty water, dodging plastic six-pack holders and soaking up enough PCBs from the bottom to give anyone's white cells more than enough reason to, what the hell, go ahead and develop cancer.

And shit, thought Bill, it was damn choppy. Their boat, a squat New York City police launch, was no lightweight. But the weird currents and a strong wind from the south had made white caps appear all over the river. It was better than the ocean to dive in, but still no picnic.

It was the other stuff he didn't like. The stuff on the bottom, the dead shit, the oyster shells that dated back to when oysters actually grew here, and fish that had puked out on too much hot water from the Indian Point nuke plant, or fresh water animals that had simply misjudged their tolerance for salt.

The eels lived, though. They might look like a dead piece of oily rope. But touch one, and "zingo," it would fly right past you, touching your fuckin' skin if you weren't lucky. Now, *that* would send a really creepy feeling right down to your balls. And they came all the way from the middle of the Atlantic Ocean just to hang out here.

Dumb fucks.

And so the boat bobbed around all morning, trying to keep on course, everyone growing bleary-eyed from the sun and staring at the sonar. Occasionally, a false blip would get them all crouching around the screen until Edward, the sonar technician who knew

130

how to read the thing, would announce it as too small, or too regular, or too something to be a body.

Which, Bill thought, was just as well. No bodies today would be just fine with him. No bodies and a little overtime to make the day's pay a clean $200. Then home to New Milford, and his wife and his son . . .

There'd been times when he got lucky and struck pay dirt. Last winter, in the East River. Some medium-big hood. A classic rub-out except the cement was around the guy's head and not his shoes. There were even signs that the punk had tried to scrape the just-drying concrete away. Nice.

Please God, thought Bill. No luck today. No . . .

"A Coke, Bill, if you're not too busy." Tom was steering the boat through the choppy water.

"Sure thing," said Bill digging a can out of the cooler bag. "Want me to spell you at the wheel?"

"Hold it there, Tom!" Edward yelled. "Hold it *right there*. I've got something. Wait a minute. Wait . . . a . . ."

Shit, thought Bill. Another five seconds and I'd be behind the wheel and it would be Tom's dive.

"Yeah. There it is. A round object, eight, maybe nine inches in diameter. Then a series of pieces crossing over each other. Could be something. It's worth a look."

Bill Eberle was already putting his tanks on. He gave his regulator a quick check, for the fifth time since getting out of bed, and grabbed his mask.

Tom had the boat alternating between an idle and quick spurts back and forth, trying to keep it in place. "You want a loot bag, old buddy?"

"No," said Bill. "I'll come up if there's something there. Just be here when I come up."

"I'll try, pal, I'll try. Just don't get lost down there."

Bill put his mouthpiece in and pulled his mask down from his forehead. He sat down on the edge of the boat and then flipped over the side.

Everything was here to turn you off to diving forever, thought Bill. Visibility about four, maybe five feet. And enough suspended crap to make it look like it was snowing in the water.

He went straight down, flipping on the lamp on his headgear as the faint sunlight quickly turned to gloom. The bottom was about fifty feet here, and he tried to estimate how far down he could swim before hitting muck. The bottom seemed to take forever to appear but then it was there, right in front of him, and he had to frantically kick his fins out to stop short.

The eels scattered, darting around him. His stomach tightened. Gotta stop this shit, he thought. It's just too damn freaky. The dull, brownish shells were everywhere, with an occasional crab sitting underneath waiting for a small fish to swim by or a bit of bologna from someone's lunch. I wonder, thought Bill, what the little fuckers think down here, behind their beady little eyes. Maybe it's just tear and chew, tear and chew, all day long.

And where the hell was the "object"? Bill wondered. He scanned right and then left, but he saw nothing except a few eels, a half-decayed flounder, a bottle.

He checked his underwater compass, tapping it,

and then swam north. He kicked five times and stopped. He scanned some more.

Nothing.

Back south again, and then five kicks further south. He looked around. Nothing.

Okay, Edward. You say it's down here. Well, where the hell is it? East?

Five kicks, and more looking around.

Something swam by.

Jesus, thought Bill. What was that? He turned to see a bit of fin and a long snout, and he remembered.

The sturgeon had returned to the Hudson River. Big mothers back to produce Hudson River caviar, if you could believe it. Probably has the beluga market shaking in its boots.

West. Five kicks. Nothing here either . . .

There.

There it is.

Sitting on top· of the shells, its color almost blending in with the oyster shells. Bingo, thought Bill. A skull. Rib bones. And who knows what other pieces mixed up in the pile.

He moved closer, shining the lamp right on the skull, staring at it real close now. Who are you, buddy? he asked the skull. The kid, the old lady, the teenager? Or are you somebody else?

The skull said nothing. But its eyes seemed to be ruminating about the question. Bill reached out to pick the skull up. His gloved hand closed around it. He lifted it up.

It moved.

He screamed then, a garbled sound, spitting his mouthpiece out, struggling to recoil in the water.

The skull was spinning free in the water now, and then landed below him.

And then, from the upside-down skull, from the hollow dish of the cranium, a fat old blue-claw crab scurried out, vacating its comfortable, dome-like abode with matching picture windows.

Shit, thought Bill sucking in his mouthpiece again. I'm getting too damn jumpy to be doing this. And now, a little angry at himself, he picked up the skull matter-of-factly and started up for the launch.

Chapter 10

Splash!

Sarah's dive into the pool was a sleek, graceful arc. She slid through the water, her sun-streaked hair flat against her head. Her strong legs kicked, moving her swiftly under the water as she opened her eyes.

She could see Shelly's legs treading water, waiting for Sarah to surface, and over to the side Patty and Christina were holding onto the pool edge. Sarah kicked some more, getting close to Shelly. She reached out, grabbed her friend's foot, and yanked.

Shelly popped down, even as Sarah shot to the surface, gulping the air. Moments later, Shelly surfaced, sputtering and wiping her eyes.

Shelly swam to the side, followed by Sarah. Then she turned to face her friend.

"Hey, Reilly, what are you trying to do? Drown me?"

"Couldn't resist," Sarah said with a smile. "I felt like a hungry shark seeing all these juicy toes dangling in the water. I just wanted to see what it felt like."

On cue, Christina, a curly-headed girl with a sea of

freckles on her face, went, "Ba-dum. Ba-dum." And then faster. "Ba-dum, ba-dum, ba-dum."

"Well, I owe you, babe. It's sneak-attack time when you're least prepared for it. Anyhow, are you sure it's no deal for the all-star sleep-over?"

Sarah turned away from the wall, her arms extending behind her, holding on to the edge of the pool. She looked out at the glistening water.

"Positively. I'm lucky to be going to the party. My parents are real nervous about all the missing people."

"Ba-dum . . . Ba-dum . . . Ba-dum, ba-dum, ba-dum," Christina sang as Shelly laughed at the theme from *Jaws*.

"Hey, my folks will be with us all the time. And Christina, Ruth, and Sharon will be there. And even Patty, right? What's a matter? Are their parents trying to get rid of them or something? It's a bummer you won't be there, S.R. It would be really radical if you were there."

"Radical?" Patty asked, and Shelly shot a look of displeasure in her direction.

"Well," said Sarah, "it's hopeless. Moving right along, what boys are coming to the party?"

"Steven, Marty, Sam, and Bradley have all said yes."

"Bradley?" Christina asked, then stuck a finger in her mouth as if to puke.

"Puh-lease," Shelly said. "Not in the pool Chlorine can do only so much. Hey look, Brad's a nice kid."

"A dork. Totally," Christina said flatly.

"I don't know. Maybe he and Patty can ge

136

something going."

Everyone turned to Patty, whose face became beet red at having her name linked with a boy.

The chattering ceased for a moment as the group awaited the arrival of the next great topic.

"You know," Christina said quietly, "I once saw Steven Parker's thing."

They all moved closer to Christina.

"Go on," Shelly said eagerly.

"Well, his parents invited my parents to a barbecue at his house. After a while, I had to pee so I went upstairs to their bathroom. I mean, I didn't know they had two bathrooms and one was downstairs. Anyhow, I went upstairs and was looking for the bathroom and I passed Steven's room. His door was open."

Sure of her audience, Christina hesitated, letting the tension rise to unbearable heights.

"And then?" Sarah asked.

"So, okay, I passed his room and he was changing into shorts or out of shorts. I don't remember. And then he turned and there it was, big as life."

"Big?" Shelly asked.

"Well, pretty big. You know, he just sort of froze there for a minute. And I said, cool as ice, 'Oh, excuse me, Steven.'"

"'And my, what a nice weenie you have,'" Shelly added, and they all laughed that wonderful belly laugh that borders on pain.

"Right," Christina said. "And how about you, Sarah? You ever see one?"

Sarah nodded, and leaped out, throwing herself off the side. She turned and faced the group, smoothly treading water. Her body felt good in the water. Light, free, all held in. Just when everything on her body felt like it was coming out. Things like the two little hills of her breasts, and her hips, and even her bottom. She was sure that it was getting larger. She had watched her mother get dressed enough times to know what a woman's body looks like. So full, rounded, something that was full of mystery. And now Sarah could see that her own rail-thin body was beginning to shift in that direction.

And then today there was this funny feeling, coming low, near her groin. Small, but definitely noticeable. And Sarah wondered whether it was her time. She was prepared for her first period, thanks to tons of filmstrips at school on the wonders of womanhood. A quiet talk with her mom one afternoon helped her know what to expect.

But still, it all scared her.

I mean, she thought, God, who wants blood oozing out of them every month?

"Who?" Christina asked with obvious interest. "Whose did you see?"

"My brother's," Sarah said with a smile. "Looks just like a little worm."

"That doesn't count," Shelly said. "And now it's time to attack!" And Shelly leaped off the side, throwing herself onto Sarah.

Shelly's weight forced Sarah down into the water. Sarah raised her hands to grab Shelly, all in fun, to pull her around and under her. And then she'd surface triumphant.

Their hands touched.

It was happening. First the slightest tremor of feeling. A faint hint of anxiety. Was Shelly's father leaving? she wondered. Was there something else she was worried about?

Then her grip tightened.

And she could see Shelly walking through her house, alone, looking for something. Looking for someone.

Looking at someone.

At the side door, in the shadows.

"Dad," she heard Shelly say.

The grip tightened, and Sarah's lungs were beginning to demand air.

"Dad." And the figure stepped out of the shadows. Stepped close to Shelly and the moonlight coming through the kitchen windows.

"Dad," she said, her voice a hollow whisper.

But it wasn't her father, it was . . .

Shelly twisted her hands away, and popped to the surface. A moment later, Sarah followed.

"Jesus, Reilly. What the hell are you trying to do? I'm keeping my distance from you in the water. You're nuts."

It was over. The sounds of the pool and the glare of the sun reflecting off the water began to erase the dark pictures in Sarah's mind. She whispered, "I'm sorry."

"Well, you should be. You know, you're pretty weird, Sarah. Sometimes, you're just too weird. Maybe it's a good thing you're not sleeping over. You could space us all out."

Sarah nodded, wishing she could explain but knowing that she shouldn't say anything.

These pictures I see, Sarah thought, I don't know what they mean. Maybe nothing.

Maybe something.

"C'mon guys, let's go back to the blankets," Christina said, trying to break the air of tension. "It's going to be time to change lifeguards soon and we gotta be in position for the show."

"Sure," Shelly muttered, and she started swimming towards the other side.

By the time it was afternoon, Shelly had forgotten the incident. They spent the rest of the day at the pool, like all others, in a seemingly endless stream of untroubled bantering.

Sarah grew more quiet as the day ended, wondering about the odd pain she felt, wondering about her friend Shelly walking through her house. . . .

And wondering, most of all, about the tall man standing in the shadows of Shelly Jaffe's kitchen.

Jack eventually had to ask Captain Merrit to ease up on the cigarettes. Breathing, Jack explained, was a priority with him.

"Okay," Merrit grunted. "All you got to do is ask."

"What I want to see," he went on, "is the places where everyone lived, where they might have been walking to, and where the streets connect together. So, Mr. Mayor, tell me where to go."

Jack led him down Patterson Avenue first. They went two blocks off Route 9, and Jack said, "That's my house."

"Nice," Merrit said perfunctorily. They passed Tompkins Street and then, as they came up to Butler,

Jack pointed left and said, "And that's Helen Waverly's place."

"Uh-huh," Merrit answered as he continued down Patterson to its end, where it met Schuyler. Jack directed him to head north.

"There," Jack announced. "That's Tommy Burdick's house." There was a bike on the front lawn lying on its side.

"Shit," Merrit said. "And nobody saw anything. Unbelievable. What do we do here?"

"Schuyler runs parallel to Route 9A. Most of the houses have some woods separating them from the highway. One block ahead is the Oakdale Nursing Home. Then you hit Butler again."

"Where's the pool?"

"Head down Butler for about four blocks."

"Okay," Merrit said. "Tommy Burdick was going to the pool so let's go there."

They drove down Schuyler, a tree-lined street of old houses with gables and roomy porches.

"Kind of secluded down here," Merrit said.

"Yeah, well, the whole neighborhood's kind of quiet."

The road became bumpy, bearing the scars of some recent sloppily patched road work.

"Been doing some digging down here?" Merrit asked.

"I guess so," Jack said. "I think there were some Con Ed trucks here a few months ago. Maybe a small gas leak or something. We had a house blow up a few years back."

"Oh yeah?"

"Sure. Some people were getting a driveway dug

141

and the bulldozer split the gas line wide open. Nobody was killed, but the house blew up like a roman candle."

"Is that the nursing home?" Merrit asked as if he wasn't listening.

"Yes. They own all the land from here until you hit Butler."

"Any head cases in there? Does it have a mental ward?"

"Not as far as I know. Just old people on their way out."

"And where did that teenager live?"

"Elliot Parks? His house is a few blocks south of the pool. We can pass it, if you like."

Merrit pulled the car to the side of the road and brought it to a stop. "Jack, would you say that you know most of the people who live around here?"

Jack shook his head. "Not really. I mean, I meet people at my store, or taking a walk. But, well, go two blocks north or south of where I live, and, for me at least, the people are strangers."

Merrit nodded. "I thought so. Here's what I want to do," he said turning toward Jack. "I'll drop you off at Town Hall. You take a couple of hours and check who's new in the neighborhood. Say, in the past few years. Take a radius of eight to ten blocks from the Waverly house."

"Is that enough?"

"Who knows? It's something to start with. Meanwhile, I'll talk to some of the families and nose around. Let's say we'll meet up at three o'clock. Then we can start looking in some of Harley's more secluded locations."

"Sure," Jack said, not relishing the idea of studying real-estate records for the next couple of hours.

The radio hissed, and a faint voice asked for Merrit. He reached over and picked up the speaker for the police radio. "Merrit here."

"Captain, the divers have found something. They're bringing it here. Do you want to come by and take a look?" Tom DeFalco sounded uncomfortable.

"What did they find, Tom?"

He heard DeFalco take a breath.

"They report a skull, and some bones. They found them about a half-mile out."

"We'll be right there," Merrit said and he put down the handpiece. "Your researching will have to wait, Jack." Merrit seemed to push the gas pedal flat to the floor, and the car screeched away. Just like in the movies, thought Jack.

No problem, he thought. How could anyone pass up seeing a skull that's been sitting in the bottom of the Hudson? He guessed he could pass up lunch today.

Merrit lit a cigarette, but Jack said nothing.

Mrs. Calvin shut the TV off.

Noah was curled up on the couch, his special blanket pulled up tight to his chin. She leaned down and felt his forehead, still warm to the touch. Poor thing, she thought. And she wondered how a mother could walk out the door with such a sick child at home. Not that Mrs. Calvin didn't have the utmost faith in her own abilities. Still a child, especially

143

such a sick child, deserved his mother.

Noah was breathing quietly, deeply asleep. What was it Julie Reilly had said? When this boy gets sick, he gets real sick. Well, he had taken some aspirin and a few gulps of juice, and there wasn't much more to do. Mrs. Calvin went out to the kitchen to make a little lunch for herself and watch "General Hospital" on the small black-and-white TV there.

While Noah dreamed.

It was the same dream. Like opening a door and, halfway open, you realize that you know what's on the other side. Sure you do. And you don't want to see it.

But it's too late.

It's already opened. And you keep pulling the door open until there it is. The dream that you know so well. The horrible, horrible . . .

Nightmare.

It started, of course, with Noah outside, playing in the sun. It was so warm, he thought. So bright and sunny. Then clouds appeared, almost as if he wasn't watching the sky carefully enough. So it changed. It wasn't sunny anymore. And it became cool.

Noah tried to pull his blanket tighter, but his feet popped out of the bottom, and he was chilled now. Outside, in the kitchen, Mrs. Calvin buttered a muffin, while an ad for Lux showed her how beautiful her hands might be.

Then, oh no, it was all cloudy everywhere, and oh so cold! Noah wanted to go inside so he ran up the front lawn thinking, when did the hill get so steep? He reached the small porch and turned to see the man.

The Tall Man, Noah called him. Please, he would

say to himself at night. Don't let me dream about the Tall Man. And sometimes he didn't. And sometimes, like now, he did.

The Tall Man waved, and Noah felt it. He smiled, thinking, how can you feel a wave? But he did and it wasn't a good feeling. It was . . .

Bad.

So Noah ran inside, and it was nice there. Warm, and cozy. Snug as a bug in a rug, his daddy always said. His mom was cooking dinner while Sarah was on the floor watching MTV. It was so nice in here, with his family. Warm and safe.

Then Noah felt it again. A chill. And he ran into the kitchen.

Mommy, Mommy, there's a man outside. A Tall Man. And he's coming in here, I just know he's coming.

And his mommy laughed—so beautiful, he thought, as she laughed. There's nobody coming in here, she said gently, there's nobody coming in at—

Then who, Noah screamed, who's that talking to Sarah?

Then Noah watched. He watched his mother run into the living room. He watched Sarah trying to struggle away from the Tall Man. And his mommy was crying, begging for someone to help. A thought occurred to Noah.

Where was Daddy?

Why wasn't he here to save us?

He watched. His mother was doubled up, crying in pain. But no one was hurting her. Where was her pain coming from? And Sarah, his bossy sister, was lying so quietly now, in the Tall Man's arms, just like a big stuffed doll. Then he carried her out, just like the movie he watched with Daddy, *The Mummy*, black and white and scratchy, with funny-looking people. But it was scary anyhow.

It's only a movie, champ, Daddy had said.

Just like . . . just like this was only a nightmare. Only a nightmare, as the Tall Man carried his sister away, and Noah cried out, his heart filled with fear, and loss, and the sheer pain of knowing he'd never see his sister again.

"Sarah," he called out. And then louder, "Sarah!"

Mrs. Calvin ran out to him and cradled his head in her full lap.

"Hush, Noah, hush. It's okay. It's a dream." Her hand, wrinkled and experienced in dealing with the woes of small children, touched his brow and felt the sweat. Noah's eyes blinked open. "There, there," Mrs. Calvin said. "See? Everything's all right. Everything's fine."

Noah said nothing, not able to tell her that she was, quite simply, wrong.

Oh yes, he thought as Mrs. Calvin turned on the TV, the Tall Man was real. 'Cause Noah had seen him right outside their house. Tonight he'd tell his daddy. And then, maybe, the Tall Man might go away.

Chapter 11

The Mid-Hudson Gallery was situated exactly at the point where Harley's Main Street met Route 9, the same Route 9 that runs from Albany to Yonkers, before entering New York City to become Broadway. Putting one foot in front of the other would indeed take an intrepid hiker from the small town of Harley to the hustling strip joints and neon glitter of the Great White Way.

When Patrick Caldwell opened his gallery, people quite naturally laughed. Downtown Harley just wasn't the kind of town for an exclusive gallery dealing in expensive fine art. It's a prison town, people snickered, a bedroom town for commuters, and people of wealth and taste wouldn't be caught dead near the uninspiring Main Street.

But the skeptics were all wrong. Harley had put together just enough "historic restoration" of its decaying turn-of-the-century shops with an emerging image as a diverse, "interesting" community to make something click. Harley had become an attractive place to visit, almost as if there was something avant-garde about a small town beset with image problems.

So, ably assisted by a pair of over-priced nouveau-cuisine restaurants, the Mid-Hudson Gallery flourished. There was even a show of prison art—dark, weirdly disturbing paintings created by multiple murderers as part of their rehabilitation.

Though not normally open until 2 p.m., the gallery was, on this morning, filled with an odd assortment of people who nibbled croissants and inspected the collection of artwork.

Julie Reilly felt out of her league here. Already she'd been grabbed by a buyer for an East Side Gallery who told her that her work lacked a certain "pain" that only living in the city could bring.

Yes, Julie had said. And I'm afraid that it's a pain I'm quite willing to forego.

She wheeled around the gallery, smiling, answering questions, examining other works on display, and feeling, through it all, inadequate.

The show was winding down when Patrick Caldwell slid next to her and gently touched her shoulder.

"They *love* your stuff, Julie. Love it."

"I'm not too sure. I don't think I'm quite esoteric enough for this crowd."

Caldwell laughed. "Just let them read what they want into your work. Depth, my dear, is in the mind of the beholder." His eyes darted to his left. "Oh, excuse me. I *must* talk to Jerome Bobbins before he gets away. Now there's what I'd call a very well-fed art maven."

She smiled thinly as Caldwell made his way over to the overweight Bobbins. She glanced up at the clock, and then walked toward the back, to Caldwell's

148

private office. She picked up his desk phone and dialed her home.

"Hello, Mrs. Calvin? How is Noah?"

There was a pause, and Julie could clearly read the rebuke in Mrs. Calvin's answer. "The same, Mrs. Reilly. Still hot and all, but he's quiet, watching his shows. Will you be back soon?"

No, Mrs. Calvin, Julie thought. I'm running away from the family forever.

"Yes. It's about over here. I imagine that another ten minutes or so should do it."

Julie turned around and she saw Caldwell come in, shutting the door behind him. He moved over to his chair, where Julie sat. She looked up at him, and he touched her hair.

"Thank you, Mrs. Calvin. I'll see you soon."

She hung up.

"Trouble?" Caldwell asked, sitting down on the edge of his desk.

Julie stood up. "Noah's sick. I feel guilty being away."

He reached out for her and pulled her close. "This show is important too," he said softly. "Miss Winant of MOMA wants a dozen pieces by November *and* the Maitland Gallery will take at least five. I'm afraid you just crossed over into the 'artist' category." Caldwell leaned forward to kiss her, but Julie turned her face and then pulled away from him.

"No, Patrick. I . . . I appreciate everything you've done for me. I mean, I'd go crazy just being a housewife." She looked right at him. "The screwing has to stop. Mark it off to my seven-year itch, pre-mid-life crisis, or whatever the hell my problem

149

was. But—"

The door opened suddenly and Jerome Bobbins stuck his porcine head in. "Oh, so sorry. Just wanted to say toodles. Nice show, Patrick. It's time you came to the city. And Miss, very nice, er, pottery." Caldwell waved goodbye as Bobbins withdrew.

"Pottery," Julie said. "So much for my new category." She walked to the door. "Thank you, Patrick. For everything. But it's just friends and business from here on, okay?"

He smiled, and Julie realized her little speech was more for herself than Caldwell. "Sure," he said. "I *value* you, Julie. As a lover, as a friend, as an artist. And whatever you're willing to share, well, that's fine." He walked up to her and grabbed her hand. "I just want you to know that this door is always open."

With a weak smile, Julie turned from him and opened the office door. She walked out through the thinning crowd of art buyers and gallery owners, and, with each step she took, she felt herself leaving the fantasy world of art and returning to the mundane world of sick children and dirty dishes in the sink.

"Yo!" Mulcahy called out to Baker, who had just come into Flanagan's Bar. "Take a seat over here. What'll you have? A bat and ball?"

Baker eyed Mulcahy's empty shot glass positioned next to a beer glass. The bartender, a short bald man with neck pouches that reminded Baker of a chubby hamster he had once owned, awaited his order.

"No. Just a beer. A light."

"Johnny, a light here for my replacement."

Baker sat down on the stool. "How's the hand?"

Mulcahy held up his hand, completely wrapped in a heavy gauze bandage. "Stings like hell. The doctor said it would be gone by today, but the pain's getting worse. But I, hah, I've been taking my own medicine."

The bartender put the beer in front of Baker and waited. Baker went for his wallet. "Oh, take it out of here," Mulcahy said, jabbing a finger down on a pile of bills in front of him. "My treat."

Baker sipped the beer slowly, not used to drinking before lunch. "This," Mulcahy said with a glance around the empty bar room, "this is a great place. A real neighborhood bar. Not any of that shitty rock music or singles shit. Just a good TV to watch the games and some nice eats on the weekends. It's a regular home away from home."

Just like Archie's Place, thought Baker. "Nice," he said, pretty sure that a bar like Flanagan's didn't get many brothers coming in off the street.

"So what did your supervisor say?"

Mulcahy held up his empty shot glass. "Another shot, Johnny, if you will. My supervisor? That bastard? He accused me of fucking up. Said I should be more careful down there and all that. I asked him, 'What's that netting stuff for?' And he said, like I was crazy or something, 'What netting?'"

"Couldn't he check with someone else? Maybe it's some kind of environmental thing. You know, to protect something or other."

The bartender poured the Four Roses with a practiced hand. Mulcahy licked his lips.

151

"Thanks, Johnny," Mulcahy said, and the bartender tapped the bar gently signaling that this one was on the house. Meaning, Baker knew, that it was number three or four. Jesus, he thought, and it's only 11 o'clock.

"No. I mean, that bastard supervisor Basilio goes off and checks with someone. Then he comes back and says that *I* was the last person to go into the damn aqueduct." He raised his left hand off the bar. "Boy, this hand's really hurting."

Baker watched Mulcahy oh-so-carefully pick up the shot glass a few inches off the bar, while his head leaned forward and his lips shaped themselves to the tiny diameter of the rim. A slurp, and half the shot was gone.

"So what now?" Baker asked. "Move on to Tarrytown?"

Mulcahy turned and looked right at the young black man. "No, my friend. Everyone says that there's nothing there, right? So if anything's there, it damn well shouldn't be, right?"

"I guess so."

"So, as the inspector of the aqueduct, I'm going to remove it. Take a look in that bag."

Baker looked down on the floor beneath Mulcahy's feet. He slid off the stool and picked it up. "Heavy," he said. "What's in here?"

"Go ahead. Take a look. Hah, one thing's for sure, I'm going out with a bang."

Baker reached in and hauled out an acetylene torch.

"What the . . ."

Mulcahy was grinning broadly, his brown teeth

152

dull in his wrinkled face. "Going to burn the shit right off the walls, Jimmy. And whatever dumb bastard put it up there is going to wish he'd told me about it. Great idea, right?"

"I dunno, man. I mean, who knows what it's for?" Baker replaced the torch.

"Who gives a shit? You and me go in there and we'll just fry right through the stuff."

Baker downed his beer, then looked at Mulcahy. "Look, man, I know you're mad but don't you think you should wait till—"

"No!" he barked. "The stuff's coming down."

"Okay, okay, but you're leaving, retiring. I just got here. I gotta work with these people. I might get fired over this. Hey, and I got a wife."

Mulcahy nodded, and then raised his near-empty glass. Someone walked in the front door, and Mulcahy gave him a wave.

"Another beer?" he asked Baker, who shook his head. "So, what's the story? You don't want to help?"

"It's not that. . . ."

"Yeah, yeah. Okay. No problem. No problem at all. I'll give you directions to the Tarrytown entrance point, you walk south, and I'll meet you there. Meanwhile I'll have cleared up the shit in Harley. Okay?"

"Sure. Just be careful. You only got one good hand."

Mulcahy laughed loudly. "But it's a damn strong hand, damn strong. Ain't that right, Bill?" The newcomer sitting at the end of the bar laughed in answer. "It will be fun. I'm gonna have one more round, then I'm going into the aqueduct. And we'll meet up at three or so. Okay, pal?"

Baker stood up. "Great. Have a good time." He laughed.

"Right. See you." And Brian Mulcahy watched Baker walk out of the small bar. Candy ass, he thought, and he breathed in, letting the rich smell of wood soaked in decades of beer and cigarette ashes fill his lungs.

"One last time, Johnny," he said. And he thought about the tunnel and the strange mesh and how good it was going to be to cut it all down.

His hand stung just then, and he wondered whether he should have the doctor take another look at it.

Then he thought, sure. Later. After he came out of the aqueduct. Plenty of time then.

He downed his last boilermaker and walked, in a surprisingly steady manner, out of the bar.

How do you deal with pain? she thought.

No, not pain. Something else. But you can't call it pain. That was easy to deal with. This, this was . . . impossible.

Catherine Burdick sat at the kitchen table, right near the phone, waiting for the call. She had played the scene out in her head many times. Hello. Yes. He's okay? My Tommy! Oh, thank God! Yes, of course. I'll be right there. And thank you, thank you.

Thank you.

But the phone just sort of sat there. And she waited wanting all the time to scream, Ring! Sweet God in heaven, ring!

154

And the moment would pass and perhaps she'd look in on the baby napping and think, guiltily, well, at least she's still here, I've still got her. They won't get her because, because . . .

Because they won't.

Ring, she pleaded, looking at the phone. Please ring.

But after the first two days, and the other missing ones, she was almost forgotten. True, the Chief called every day just to say that there was no news, and she could sense his eagerness just to be off the phone. And her few friends seemed unable to stay very long with her, as if what had happened to her was somehow contagious.

She cried quietly, letting it go now, just a little now, since the baby was asleep. She could be strong the whole day, except for now, when she was all alone.

She cried, but the tears no longer flowed. A few drops and then her eyes just took on a sad, dead expression that would slowly become the new way she looked. Mrs. Burdick went to the sink and the breakfast dishes (not as many as there used to be) and turned on the faucet. A double window over the sink looked out to the backyard where she could see . . .

Tommy.

"No," she whispered. It wasn't possible. She blinked, and he was still there. He smiled, his long shiny brown hair threatening to cover his blue eyes. He laughed and then he waved at her.

She rushed to the side door, her mind singing sweet praises to God, and she ran out to the backyard. But there was no one there.

155

"Tommy!" she called loudly. "Tommy, come out! I know you're back here. I'm not angry, honey. Please, baby," she said, her voice almost crying now, "where are you?"

And then she saw him pop his freckled face out of the back hedges next to the Wileys' house. He giggled.

"Come here, Tommy," she pleaded. But he disappeared into the bushes. Catherine Burdick ran to him, but her lungs forced her to slow. She was sweating heavily as she reached the hedges.

She couldn't see him in the lush, green bushes. Suddenly, from the Wileys' driveway, she heard his voice.

"Hi, Mom! Want to play freeze-tag?"

She thought of her baby lying asleep back at the house.

"Tommy, sweetheart, please come back. I'm not mad, honey. Just please come here."

He laughed again and dashed away, down the driveway, out across the street, across Schuyler Road.

Catherine Burdick pushed her way through the hedge. He was getting away, leaving her again. She couldn't let that happen, couldn't stand the pain.

She moved, a clumsy, slow-footed thing, puffing and sweating, her body groaning from excess weight as she hurried to the street.

There he was, walking away from her now. He moved slowly, as though he was just taking a walk in the hot midday sunlight of summer. Surely she could catch up to him now, she thought. She ran across the street, struggling to reach her son.

He turned around, and grinned that full-faced,

toothy smile that flashed whenever he played a trick on his mom. Then he darted away, skipping, letting his hand trail along a wood fence.

"Tommy," she yelled. "Stop it now. I mean it!" Then, crying, "Tommy, please stop running!"

But he cut up the driveway of a big white house halfway down Schuyler.

The large house had heavy columns in front, and a generous porch that spread out of its front and wrapped around both sides. Catherine Burdick barely saw it, her eyes on her son. There was a back door. Tommy seemed to be looking into it. Then he entered the house.

She followed. Now, she thought at last, now I'll have my boy back. And I'll hold him and kiss him and never lose him again. If I could just get him back.

She entered the back door and paused. She heard his giggle come from downstairs. She walked down, to the basement.

There. Right in front of her. Smiling, licking his lips from his run.

"Oh, Tommy. My sweet baby." Her arms went out to hold him, to press him into her body.

But Tommy's smile faded, a confused look crossed his face. And then he was gone. In his place was a man, tall, thin, dressed in a gray suit.

She stepped back. Had she imagined the whole thing? Had she just walked into this stranger's house? She felt embarrassed, disoriented. . . .

"Oh, I'm sorry," she muttered. "I . . . I thought my son . . . my son."

Yes, he said. Your son is here.

"What?" she whispered. Her lips began to tremble.

157

Your son is here, Mrs. Burdick. Behind you.

She turned.

She screamed as her eyes took in the sickening image before her. There were hands, each one somehow opening and shutting, acting more like hungry mouths. And then she looked up and saw some kind of head, with dark, bottomless eyes that made her stomach twist with an insane, hopeless fear. She wet herself.

"No," she moaned.

Now you can join your son, the man seemed to say quietly, so quietly that there was no sound. And the thing reached out for her with one of its hands. It seemed to attach itself to her chubby arm with a sick, sucking sound, and then it snapped her body quickly forward. With one final howl, Catherine Burdick vanished from the small basement room.

The tall man walked to the curtains on the floor and carefully scooped them up. He replaced them on the mirror. He smiled, knowing that his work was almost done. Two more days, and the time would be here.

After that, he knew, nothing would ever be the same again.

Chapter 12

Merrit turned the skull over, scrutinizing it carefully. His eyes squinted, his lips pursed. He passed it rather gingerly to Jack.

"Too bad," he said. Then, turning to DeFalco, "You sent the divers out again prontissimo, I assume?"

"And none too happily," DeFalco said.

Merrit raised his eyebrows. "Jittery, eh? Well, they're young and well paid. Let's not worry about their nerves."

Jack held the skull awkwardly at first. It was cradled in his hands, as he half-listened to the conversation and thought . . .

This was once the command center of a *person*, the place that said hi and gave orders to the legs and arms, read books, laughed. Cried.

He turned it over and looked into the hollows of the eyes. The skull's crazed grin clashed with the shadowy, lost look of the eye sockets.

"Too bad about what?" Jack asked, almost as an afterthought.

Merrit reached over and took the skull.

"This," he said, "is a very nice specimen, but it has absolutely nothing to do with the cases. At least, the current ones." He placed the skull down on the blotter of DeFalco's desk with a thud.

"How do you know?" Jack asked.

"See the tiny holes on the surface? And there, to the side, the greenish color? That's algae. There's these tiny worms that live in the river and they can eat through skulls, bone, any porous material. I'm afraid that this skull's been in the Hudson for a couple of months. Maybe more."

"Months?" Jack said. "Then who is it?"

"We're checking on it," DeFalco answered.

"Happens all the time," Merrit said. "We come up with the bones to some other murder. Well, enough time wasted. I'm going to talk to the families of the missing people, and nose around the neighborhood some more. And you . . ."

"I know. Real-estate records at the Town Hall," Jack said without enthusiasm.

"Precisely," Merrit said with a broad smile.

Cheerful bastard, thought Jack. Just like this is some kind of picnic. He shrugged and walked out of DeFalco's office.

Catherine Burdick's neighbor, a middle-aged woman named Florence Kendall, heard the baby crying, a cat-like sound that somehow blended eerily with the noisy cicadas.

At first she ignored it. The sound of crying kids was just one of those things you heard. Just like the occasional family quarrel that spilled through the

160

open windows, with people screaming at each other.

So Florence Kendall went on with her household chores.

But the crying didn't stop. In fact, it grew more desperate.

Finally, Florence Kendall went next door, to the back screen door, and tapped on it. "Catherine? Is there anything wrong?" she called through the wire-mesh screen. The kitchen was empty.

Florence Kendall knew the terrible things that must be going through Catherine Burdick's head, what with Tommy gone and everything. Anything, she thought grimly—her imagination fired by television movies with distraught mothers trying to kill themselves—yes, anything was possible.

"Catherine?" she called louder, but the only sound was the baby's horrible, rhythmic screaming. Florence Kendall opened the screen door, stepping into the usually neat house, now bearing signs of neglect.

She kept calling Catherine's name as she made her way upstairs, to the baby's room.

The baby girl, Tammy, was standing up in her crib, her face streaked with the dried trails of tears.

"There, there," Kendall cooed, remembering her many afternoons calming her own three youngsters. "Did you just wake up?" she said gently, picking the girl up.

"There, that's better, isn't it?"

She carried Tammy downstairs, all the time wondering—

Where is her mother?

Tammy had finally stopped crying. Now she was

just sniffling in the afterburn of her hysterics.

"How about a few cookies and some juice?" Kendall said, putting Tammy down on the floor. She searched the cabinets, coming up with a nearly empty bag of Oreos. She found a can of Welch's grape juice in the refrigerator and poured some in a cup. Then, thinking better of it, she dumped the contents of the cup into a plastic baby bottle.

"There you go," she said brightly, giving the girl the bottle and a plate of cookies. "Now, I'll see if I can find your mommy."

She checked the entire house, even poking her head through the basement and attic doors to call out Catherine Burdick's name. A creepy feeling came over her.

You don't leave a one-and-a-half-year-old alone.

She picked up the phone and called the police.

A squad car was outside in minutes and Tom DeFalco hurried out, up to the house.

As Florence Kendall let the Police Chief in, the baby was playing quietly on the floor.

"I've asked the father to come here," DeFalco said quietly.

"I just *had* to come in." Florence looked down at Tammy, who was stacking alphabet blocks on top of each other. "I mean, if you could have heard the screaming."

DeFalco pulled a kitchen chair out for Florence to sit on. He noticed that her hands were playing with a napkin, twisting it this way and that, curling it around her fingers.

"You didn't see Mrs. Burdick leave the house?"

"No. I mean, I'm not nosy or anything. People

162

have their own lives. I know she's been under a great—"

"So you didn't see anything?" DeFalco interrupted. Kendall shook her head.

The front door opened and Mr. Burdick entered the house.

"Great," he said looking around. "Bitch loses one kid, leaves the other. What a winner!"

DeFalco walked over to Burdick, smelling a slight aroma of beer on his breath. "You don't have any idea where your wife might be, do you, Mr. Burdick?"

"No way. Hey, I was at work all morning. Don't try to lay this one on me."

"No one's trying to lay anything on you, Mr. Burdick."

Tammy stood up and walked over to Florence. Burdick turned to her. "Hey, sweetie, give your daddy a hug?"

The girl pulled tighter against Florence.

DeFalco went over to Florence Kendall and said, very quietly, "Would you be able to take care of the girl, at least until we can make other arrangements with Social Services?"

Florence seemed startled by the request. "I . . . well, I don't know. It's been a long time since . . ." Tammy then pulled the twisted napkin from the woman's hand and grabbed one of her fingers tightly. Florence looked at her. "Yes," she said. "Certainly. At least until . . ."

"Wait a second," Burdick barked out. "I'm the kid's father and I should decide where she goes. My sister in Flushing can . . ."

163

DeFalco quickly pulled Burdick back, out to the living room. "She's a frightened little girl, Mr. Burdick. Don't you think it would be better if she could stay near her house, with her toys and clothes nearby?"

"I don't know," Burdick said warily. DeFalco looked him right in the eye, both a warning and a challenge. "Sure," Burdick said. "I guess so."

"Good." DeFalco smiled.

When he walked out to his car, he called into the station to add one more name to the list of people who had disappeared from the quiet town of Harley-on-Hudson.

"Hey, mister. You goin' in there again?"

Mulcahy turned, trying to locate the kid's voice. Just behind him was a thin black boy, shirtless and standing about five yards away. Mulcahy shifted the heavy bag he was carrying, trying to make the awkward load balance better.

"Whaddya mean 'again,' kid? Maybe you saw me yesterday?"

The kid shook his head.

"No, I saw the people this morning. They didn't see me 'cause I hid. And I didn't see anyone who looked like you." He paused. "You goin' in there again?"

The air took on a wobbly, washed-out heaviness. Mulcahy wondered whether it was the heat, or maybe his tolerance for booze was just not what it used to be. He felt like he could be sick, right there, and the kid would watch him toss his cookies all over the browned-out grass.

"No, son. There was no one here this morning. We were here yesterday." Mulcahy turned and walked to the entrance plate, looking forward to the cool darkness of the tunnel.

Behind him, the boy watched.

"Was too," he said quietly. "I saw people go in there today." But Mulcahy was already prying the heavy grating open, struggling to lift it with his one good arm.

Wide-eyed, the boy watched the fat man disappear down the tunnel, just like a well-fed raccoon scurrying down a sewer. Mulcahy pulled the grating behind him. The boy watched until it was over and then skipped happily away.

Lines. Lines. Lines.

Eli Singer tried to bear this in good humor. He looked up to a balcony to see airport security guards scanning the crowd of people as they approached the U.S. Customs counters. He remembered that at one time the balcony was open to people awaiting international arrivals. But then there were stories about bribed customs officials and hand signals directing travelers with drug-laden suitcases to move to a certain line.

So now the security police looked down, impassive, bored, watching the lines.

But these weren't sad lines, thought Singer. There was nothing bad here, nothing . . . evil.

People here were going someplace, looking forward to something. Family, lovers, a new job, a nice hotel. It was America. Another 100 feet and it was America.

He looked over at the people in the line to his right. A baby girl slept on her daddy's shoulder, while the father's face showed his own growing fatigue from holding her. Over the man's other shoulder was a bag pulling down, digging into him, probably loaded with diapers, a bottle, some toys. A small boy clutched his mother's leg. He looked bleary-eyed from the traveling even as his mother ran her hand through his curly brown hair. She would take a few steps forward with a bag and then put it down until the next gap opened before her.

They were returning home, Singer thought. Dreaming now of their suburban home and their big comfortable beds. Happy to come home to America.

How different, Singer thought. How amazingly different from other lines. Lines that took people nowhere. Lines to no place. Lines to oblivion.

He stepped forward.

Without wanting to, he watched the family and remembered.

His village was fifty kilometers east of Warsaw. It was called Bransk Podlaski. Large enough to have a big main square with a red-brick town hall, and small enough so that Eli could bicycle from one end to the other in ten minutes.

He was seventeen. His family had warned him to be careful. The German soldiers had seemed friendly enough in their triumphant, lightning march east. But people spoke darkly of other soldiers, those who would come later, following in their sleek gray trucks that roared into towns in the middle of the night.

And then what? Eli had laughed. Lock all the Jews up? Why, that would be half the village. No, he said, wise in the ways of modern warfare. It was *Russia*, the great Bolshevik menace, that the Nazis were after. Not the middle-class Jews of Bransk Podlaski.

They came at night, fulfilling the prophecy of the few old fools who spoke of other pogroms and feared the worst was yet to come. The trucks pulled into the square and soldiers emptied from them, their boots clattering on the street, machine guns held tightly in their fists. The word spread through the village much faster than Eli's bike ever did.

SS.

Soon they were at his door, snapping in German, "Kommen!" and gesturing for them to get out. And when they did, grabbing a light jacket to warm themselves against the light chill of late summer, they joined the others, joined them in one great line.

Some tried to make light of it. Just some kind of registration process, they said. But when the SS "Special Action" squads began to smash their machine gun butts into the skulls of anyone who talked, everyone became quiet.

One young man turned and ran. They fired. Even in the darkness the man's blood glistened on the cobblestones. There was weeping, then, as the line swelled and mothers tried to quiet their scared, crying children. The old people trudged stoically.

They'd seen it before. And, as they walked, they felt that they'd live to see it again.

The line wound through the center of town, then moved out of the village to the thick woods that bordered the clear waters of the Wita River.

Eli's breath came in short, shallow gasps as the ghostly line moved further out, further away from the town, from homes, from civilization. Where, everyone wondered, some whispering to neighbors, where are we going? To a camp? To some place for interrogation? Where? Where?

They stopped. They waited. Suddenly the night exploded with the sound of machine guns firing. A crazy burst of sound. The line moved forward. Eli looked at the people around him. What should we do? he wondered, his panic growing. Dear God, he thought, what is happening? But no one answered his silent question. And the line moved on.

Finally, he reached a place where many soldiers stood. Someone counted off twenty people from the front of the line. Eli was eighteenth. "Achtzehn." The sound of the soldier's voice saying the word would stay with him forever. The rest were told to wait. They marched the group straight ahead, up and over a small hill.

Now the moaning and crying filled the night. A young woman fell to her knees. A soldier came and crashed his rifle down onto her. He kicked her. She slowly, desperately struggled back to a standing position.

The soldiers were shouting now too. "Schnell!" they screamed. Hurry up, move the line along. Keep moving. Move!

Until the twenty were standing in front of a pit about five meters by ten meters, a pit filled with bodies, some of them still moving, calling out. The twenty watched the pit in horror, even as the machine guns suddenly cut them down, slicing them from the earth and tumbling them down into the still-living pit.

Eli took three shots. One in his shoulder. Another entered his back a little above his waist. The third entered his thigh. He fell into the pit.

More people arrived, more shots, more people, more shots, bodies falling upon bodies, a human death harvest. The people on top were suffocating those below. The weight on Eli grew unbearable. He moved his arm to create a pocket to protect his mouth and nostrils from the press of flesh and the blood dripping down.

At that moment, he had but one goal.

To live. To somehow survive to tell the world. To bear witness to this evil.

And yes, to avenge it.

Like all lines, this one too had an end. When they were done, the SS stomped on top of the pile, shooting into those still living, sealing in those below with a cap of dead bodies. . . .

"Please put your bag up here, sir."

Singer looked at the young woman at the Customs desk.

"Anything to declare?" she asked. He shook his head.

She opened his bag. He watched her quickly feel its

169

corners, pushing against his few articles of clothing. She felt a book, picked it up, replaced it. To her the book was a foreign work, with an unpronounceable title.

"Thank you," she said. "Next?"

Singer exited into the terminal. The bright, glaring lights and hurrying people disoriented him.

A car, he remembered. He went to the Hertz desk, where a man in a yellow vest took Singer's credit card and gave him a receipt. He directed Singer to take a shuttle bus to Parking Area 7, where he would find a blue Chrysler waiting for him.

He concentrated now, tired as he was, on finding the shuttle bus and getting to Hertz's lot. In fifteen minutes he was driving his car out of Kennedy Airport. He dug a map out of his coat pocket. It was folded carefully to expose his route marked in red.

I wish, he thought, I wasn't so tired. I wish I was young.

He glanced at the map. A big red circle surrounded a town called Harley. He reached into his other pocket. My pills, he thought. I'm late taking them. And that's not good. I can't be careless now. It's too important.

And, as he drove along the Belt Parkway, nearing the Verrazano Bridge, he shut the windows and flipped on the air conditioner. Then he let himself finish the memory. Because, he knew, if not then, it would surely finish in his dreams. . . .

How long had he lain there, bleeding near the top of the mass grave? He didn't know. Gradually, there were fewer moans. He could feel his own blood still pouring out of him. Soon I'll be dead, he thought. And maybe that's what I want.

He became aware of the smell, an animal smell of death and carnage. He pictured himself lying there, not moving, melting into the pit. He reached out, forcing his hand up, touching here an open wound, there a face beyond caring about his unwanted intimacy. His fists closed around someone's leg. He pulled himself upward. A little at a time. He kicked, trying to swim in the human sea, thrusting himself forward.

He prayed constantly. He prayed for strength, he prayed for revenge, he prayed for sanity.

His body was lean, lanky. He squeezed it through the human tide until, unbelievably, his fingertips could feel nothing. No more bodies.

The air, his mind whispered.

He grew cautious. They may have guards posted. He waited, his head pressed against a woman's rounded belly, listening for sounds.

The woods seemed alive with ravens. It wasn't until later that Eli would know why. Breezes rustled through the nearby oak trees. Eli heard nothing else, and he sensed his own growing weakness.

He clawed his way out now, growing almost giddy when his blood-streaked face popped out of the human mound. He struggled and kicked the last few feet, until he suddenly popped out. Then he crawled over the bodies, sending the feasting ravens scattering in all directions, before breaking into a run toward the woods.

He barely noticed that he limped, or that his left

side was giving him intense pain. He ran as fast as he could, almost thinking that it was all some kind of death dream, a delusion, while he was actually gulping his last fetid breath among the hundreds of dead Jews in the pit.

But no, he told himself, he was alive. Before long he stopped running. He fell to the ground, sobbing like a baby. He cried for his life that was over, and his life yet to come. He wondered whether being a survivor was a blessing or a curse. . . .

New York. It seemed to appear all at once. He could see the East Side skyline, then the bridges from Brooklyn to Manhattan. He rubbed his moist eyes.

A cab next to him blared its horn, the driver shooting him a dirty look. Singer looked at the speedometer. It read twenty-five miles an hour.

I must stop and concentrate, he thought. I can't allow myself to get lost, to let myself think of other things.

The city was shrouded before him, a magic kingdom of towers and spires surrounded by water and a hazy afternoon mist. He thought of the people. So many people, he thought, so many, so close together.

Are there ravens in New York? he wondered.

He pressed harder against the accelerator.

Chapter 13

The first thing Mulcahy did was switch on his lamp. He had to fiddle a moment before he found the toggle switch. Then he placed his canvas bag down on the tunnel floor. Bending over, he picked up the bag and pulled out the acetylene torch. When he stood up with it, he felt more than a little dizzy.

He looked down the long tunnel.

At first his alcohol-befuddled mind didn't register any changes. But once his doubts were overcome, he realized that, yes, it was different.

There's more of it, he thought. The webbing stretched as far as he could see. He started walking slowly south, down the tunnel, but there seemed no end to it. For the first time, he wondered whether he could manage cutting it all down.

He laughed out loud then, a hollow-sound echoing in the damp tunnel. Well, he figured he could certainly cut down a whole lot of the shit, whatever it was.

He licked his lips. He'd like another drink, and he was annoyed that he hadn't brought something to wet his whistle while working. A few beers would have done nicely, he thought. Maybe a pint of Four Roses.

Then Mulcahy noticed the second change.

It was on the webbing itself, some kind of coating that glistened as the small lamp sprayed it with a pale light. At first, it looked like dew. Yeah, Mulcahy thought, just like tiny droplets of dew. Maybe, he figured, maybe the moisture in here, somehow or other . . .

But no. He stepped close to the webbing. But not too close, he reminded himself. There was a tiny globe of something or other supported by a few strands of the prickers. Mulcahy leaned in for a closer look. The globes looked clear, apparently empty. They reminded him of something, something that he saw a long time ago. When he was a kid. Something he saw near the surface of his uncle's pond . . .

He heard a sound.

His heart picked up a slightly faster pace. The sound. It was just like . . .

What?

A step, maybe? He stood still and listened. There it was again. A step. Someone else was here. But who?

Oh, yeah. He smiled.

"Baker?" he yelled out. "That you, Jimmy?" Mulcahy waited for an answer, his smile slowly melting from his face. He tried to aim the light back to the north, where the sound came from, past where the webbing stopped. Nothing.

He waited, but the sound had stopped. His mind searched for other possibilities.

Bats. They're all over the place. "Sure," he said to himself. "Just some bats flapping around." Well,

174

don't you worry little fellas, he thought, 'cause I'm going to clean your house. And maybe fry a couple of you in the process.

He dug into his coat pocket and put on his welding goggles. The tunnel's darkness was now covered by the smeary film on the scuffed-up goggles. For a moment he wasn't sure he could even see well enough to cut the webbing. But after a moment's disorientation, he realized that he could see just enough to move around. And he knew that he sure as hell would be able to see the torch.

There were three steps to lighting the torch. First, a safety switch had to be thrown on. Then the gas valve itself was opened, while a flint igniter was hit. He moved quickly, fearing he was losing his taste for the work at hand. The torch sparked to life, sputtering, sending a sword-like flame in front of him. He adjusted the flow of gas. The flame became smaller.

It filled the tunnel with an electric, crackling sound. Now he could cut through the webbing like it was pizza cheese.

Mulcahy stepped close to the wall on his left. He raised the torch to it. All he could hear was the erratic spitting sound of the torch as he began to cut.

Something wrapped around his ankle.

Then he felt that pain. Oh sweet God the pain, as a hundred needles entered his skin, and pierced his bones and tendons. He screamed and looked down to see a thick strand of the stuff coiled around his white socks, which were slowly turning a deep crimson.

It was an incredible anger he felt, as he sliced down with the torch to cut that strand. Had he stumbled upon it, he wondered, or was some of it just lying around? He asked himself this question as his good arm brought the torch down.

But it never made it.

Another strand was somehow suddenly around his right wrist, squeezing tight, driving the needles into his skin. Then, his other arm was held tight. Then, the other ankle. And Mulcahy screamed.

"Help! Someone, please help me!"

He pulled against it, knowing that it held him fast. The strands pulled even tighter, and the lamp fell limply from his hands into the small pool of water at his feet. Then, at last, a strand went around his neck.

"No," he moaned. "Please, no."

But it coiled slowly around his chunky, fat-laden neck before it tightened. Mulcahy's screams startled bats sleeping over a mile away.

It was then that he saw a face.

A woman, short and puffy-faced, looking at him as though he were some exhibit in a museum. And Mulcahy tried to form the word "Help," but his lips merely opened and blood gurgled out onto the stone floor.

The webbing tightened. Mulcahy, now dead, was pulled fast to the wall. He stood out like a trophy on a hunter's wall. But in a few hours, when the lamp's batteries failed, he'd blend in with the red bricks, and the moss, and the glistening webbing.

Outside, playing in a dead maple tree, climbing out onto a rotten limb, a small, shirtless boy thought he heard something. A cry maybe. He stopped climbing. Hearing nothing, he continued testing himself against the old tree.

*   *   *

"Miller time, Reilly." Merrit startled Jack as he suddenly appeared by the metal desk near the dozens of file cabinets that held the town's records. "Finished?" he asked.

Jack shook his head. He was starting to like Merrit. A little levity might just be what's needed to do this kind of work. "About halfway done, I guess," he answered. "You know, this doesn't cover any new renters or transients bedding down in Mrs. Phelan's boarding house. And who says it has to be someone new to Harley?"

Merrit pulled up a folding chair. "True enough, but what you're doing will help us check one group, new homeowners. And chances are, whoever's doing this didn't start it a week ago." Jack saw Merrit eye the "No Smoking" sign. He picked up a paper clip off the desk and began twisting it. "No, my guess is that they did something like this before, most likely somewhere else."

"Could be. Look Captain, I . . ."

"Lee, Jack. It's Lee."

Jack smiled. "Right. Well, I've got to get home. I'll finish this tomorrow, okay?" Merrit nodded, and Jack slapped a big register book closed. "I'll have Emily open the store again tomorrow."

Merrit walked Jack out of the Town Hall and down to his black patrol car. "Boy," he said stopping in the hot evening sun, "it just gets hotter and hotter."

"That's summer for you," Jack said dryly. Then, as they both got into the car, "Did you learn anything interesting this afternoon?"

Merrit started the car and pulled out of the small parking lot. "Sure did. I learned that you've got a lot

177

of scared people out there. And the father of Elliot Parks was pretty obnoxious. He told me that the cops in this town weren't worth a damn." Merrit looked at Jack. "I disagreed with him, of course."

Merrit grew quiet and Jack quickly sensed that there was something he wasn't saying.

"What's up, Lee? You're not telling me something."

"It's that easy to tell, eh? Well, Jack, Tommy Burdick's mother is gone. The baby was crying, the door open. . . ."

"Jesus. This is getting to be too much."

"Agreed. Anyhow, tomorrow I'm going to your prison to see what wonderful reformed citizens they've unleashed lately."

Merrit turned down Patterson towards Jack's house. "Jack," he said, "keep an eye on your family. We have a half-dozen state troopers helping your police, who are already working overtime. And we still have doodley-squat. It's best you be careful."

"I have been, Lee. Just ask my daughter."

Merrit stopped the car in front of Jack's house. "I'll stop by Town Hall to pick up the list around noon, okay?" Jack started to get out. "Oh, can you keep Sunday open?"

"I guess so," answered Jack. "Why?"

Merrit lit a cigarette and sucked in a luxurious gulp of smoke. "I've made an appointment with a woman who lives in the Bronx, near Fordham Road. She teaches kindergarten in some public school near there."

Merrit paused. "Okay," Jack said, "I'll bite. Why are we going to see her?"

178

Merrit looked right at Jack, his eyes adding a force to his words that left Jack a bit unsettled. "She's a psychic. She helped me zero in on William Barstow. You know, the Buffalo housewife killer? Now, there was a sweet guy." He took a drag of his cigarette. "She's the genuine article, Jack. It doesn't work all the time. I don't know what the deal is, but . . ."

"You want me to go along?"

"Yeah. You knew the victims, some of them at least. And personal contact is important for her. She can ask you questions about them. I'm also bringing some of their personal effects. It helps her." A long ash from Merrit's cigarette landed rather conspicuously on his dark pants. "So, Sunday, nine a.m. okay? Lunch on me at White Castle. Okay?"

"Sure." Jack laughed.

Jack got out of the car. Before the door was shut, Merrit leaned over. "Keep this under your hat, okay? It just wouldn't look good in the local papers."

"Gotcha. Have a nice night, Captain." Jack shut the door and watched Merrit drive away.

Noah was curled up on the couch, his eyes half-open, as he watched "Dangermouse."

"Hey, guy," Jack said going over to him. "How're you feeling?"

"Good," Noah said quietly. Jack put his hand up to his son's brow.

"You're still hot, tiger. Let me go say hi to the rest of the family, then I'll come back and sit with you."

Noah nodded. Jack walked out to the kitchen, where a thin smoke hung in the air.

179

Julie was carefully laying strips of fish in the frying pan and quickly pulling her hand back from the snaps and crackles of the hot oil. Jack came behind her and pulled her close.

"Thair ees something fishy hair, no?" he said in his best imitation of Inspector Clouseau. Julie turned to kiss him full on the mouth, both of them making peace from the morning. His hands went to her bottom and pulled her tight.

"Boy," he said, "police work makes me horny."

"Let me get the rest of the flounder in or we'll be eating in shifts," she laughed.

"I don't think Noah will be eating at all."

"Poor kid." Julie moved back to the frying pan. "I took him to the doctor as soon as I got back from the gallery. He said it was a virus. It just has to run its course. . . ."

"If it runs anymore," Jack snapped, "we're taking him to another doctor. A fever shouldn't be lasting this long."

He waited while she placed the rest of the filets in the pan. "There," she said. "Emily said everything went fine at the store."

"And how'd things go at the gallery?"

"Great. I can sell just about as much as I can make . . . and at New York prices."

"Super. We can certainly use the extra money."

"Oh," Julie said, glancing at the clock. "'Jeopardy' is on." She reached over to turn on the small TV on what Noah called "the cereal shelf."

"My God!" Jack said, raising his hands in horror. "And to think you almost missed it. Where's Sarah?"

"In her room. Moping." She turned to glance at

the TV screen. "Secretary of State under Nixon. Wasn't that Kissinger?"

The "Jeopardy" host, Alex Trebek, announced that indeed it was Henry Kissinger. Julie turned to Jack. "She's a bit upset. All her friends are sleeping over, she said. Everyone but her."

"I'll go see if I can soothe the savage beast."

Jack went upstairs to Sarah's room and faced the shut door adorned with Bruce Springsteen's *Born in the U.S.A.* poster, vividly displaying Bruce's jeans-covered buttocks.

"Sarah," he said as he tapped the door gently. Then he opened, having observed the proprieties of pre-teen privacy.

She was spread out on her bed reading a book. Jack sat down next to her thinking, I'm doing a lot of parenting a la Robert Young this evening.

Her room was kept neat. He saw all her plush animals at their assigned posts, their glass eyes keeping a sharp lookout for any sign of intruders. Sarah's desk top was empty awaiting next year's math homework and inevitable social studies reports. (Jack hoped he never heard of Paraguay again.) While Noah's room was a bomb site, this was a set out of a Spielberg movie.

"Pretty mad, huh?"

"No," she said flatly. "It's just that, well, everyone's going. *Everyone*. It's just not fair."

Jack touched her silky hair. Already she wasn't really his anymore. Already she had her own special friends, her own world, and he was just some stubborn anchor holding her fast to the family and the house. It all goes by too quickly, he thought.

181

"This 'missing person' business will be over soon," he said. "And then you can go on all the sleepovers you want. You understand that, don't you, Sarah?"

She looked at him, dubious. "I guess so. It's just that it's going to be so much fun."

And you're only almost-twelve once in your life, Jack knew. He stood up. "So, I tell you what we'll do. I'll rent a bunch of cassettes for tomorrow night, after the party, maybe something really creepy like *Halloween IV*."

"Mom won't watch that," she said laughing.

"You're right there. But you and I can."

He leaned over and kissed her cheek. He walked out of the room, and down to Noah. He sat down beside him on the couch. The end titles for the cartoon were on.

"Dangermouse did it again, eh?" Jack asked.

Noah nodded.

"What's on next?"

"I don't know," Noah answered in a throaty whisper. He pulled his blanket tighter. Then, he turned his head to face his father.

Jack watched the next show begin. "Oh, it's Lassie. What a dog, huh?" He turned. Noah was looking at him. He was crying.

"Hey, hey, buddy. What's wrong?" Noah crawled out from his blanket to lay his head on his father's lap. "There, it's okay. You're just a little sick. By tomorrow—"

"I saw him, Daddy. I saw the Tall Man."

Jack gave Noah a funny look. "The Tall Man? Who's the Tall Man?"

"He's some man, Daddy. I've dreamed about him. He comes to our house and takes—"

"Whoa! Hold on a minute. That's a dream, Noah. Just a dream. And you know, dreams aren't real."

The boy nodded.

"Dinner!" Julie called.

"I'll get you some food," Jack said. He started to stand up.

Noah's small hand grabbed two of Jack's fingers and held tight. "I saw him, Daddy. I saw him . . . for real."

Jack sat down. "What are you saying, Noah? Saw who?"

Noah's hand squeezed the fingers as he talked. He's scared, thought Jack. Absolutely terrified. And his hand, why, now it's almost cold.

Noah spoke solemnly, as if revealing a secret. "Yesterday, I looked out the window and he was there. Watching. Watching our house. Then he saw me and I went away from the window."

"Wait a minute, you saw someone outside our house? And you think he wants to come in?" Noah nodded. Jack fought to keep a look of fear from his face. "It was probably just someone taking a walk, Noah. That's all. You shouldn't worry about it."

But even as he was reassuring his son, something clicked inside Jack. It was like when you hear someone's bad news, he thought. And all the time you're giving them sympathy and encouragement, secretly, inside, you breathe a sigh of relief.

At least it's not me.

I didn't lose my kid. It happened to someone else. And doesn't it always happen to someone else?

Or, he now wondered, does it?

"The man watched our house?" Jack tried to ask in a casual way. Noah's small head bobbed again. "A tall man?" he asked. "And what else?"

"That's all, Daddy. Tall. With mean eyes."

"Well, don't worry, champ. I'll make sure no one comes in here." He stood up. "It was probably just someone out for a stroll, that's all. Now, let me get you some food."

Noah's daddy went out to the kitchen to fix Noah a plate of fish and french fries. . . .

And he'd ask Noah's mommy about any strangers seen around the house. . . .

And Noah would try to remember, try to remember to tell his daddy the worst part.

The Tall Man's not a man at all. No, Noah had to say. I've seen him in my dreams. The Tall Man's really, really . . .

A monster.

And he's coming back.

a big plate of eggs and hash browns, others to cap the evening with a few brews at Joe Whalen's Bar and Grill.

Merrit turned to look at the now very still lake, so clearly reflecting the full moon.

Then he saw the tiny bit of movement across the lake, near the top of one of the sheer cliffs.

"Wait," Merrit ordered. The few remaining cops stopped in their tracks. "There's someone over there!"

Merrit was already moving, running along the edge of the lake, towards the cliff.

"Follow him," the captain ordered his cops.

As Merrit ran, he watched the progress of the person on the cliff. He had hid himself just below the top of the cliff, in a small fissure. With the moon behind him, he'd be in the shadows until he moved. A precarious position but not a place anyone would ever likely check.

The figure was up now, over the edge, probably making his way through the woods behind. The captain was on his walkie-talkie ordering the various police cars back.

But Merrit knew that if he didn't get to him, the "Meat Man" would be gone.

His breath started to go, and Merrit cursed himself for smoking. His oxygen debt came due and he was gulping down air.

When he reached the trail leading up to the ridge that ran alongside the cliff, Merrit took his gun out, knowing exactly what he'd do if he got there in time.

Please God, he thought, let me just get to him.

But as he ran, he became aware of a tremendous

stillness that filled this heavily wooded area.

Possible trails seemed to stretch in all directions, 360 degrees of escape routes.

He held his gun foolishly in his hand. It was all over. Once again, the "Meat Man" had escaped.

And still, Merrit thought, looking now at Harley Prison and puffing his cigarette down to the last smokable millimeter, he was still free today.

Somewhere.

He flipped the cigarette down, looked at the prison wall, "The Big House" up the river.

Well, he thought, having made one loop around the sandy-colored fortress, looking for the entrance, perhaps it was time to get some assistance.

Merrit went to his police radio and called into the station for some help. He scribbled the directions down on the sheet of paper with the warden's name, Michael Grossbach.

He turned on the civilian radio and heard the cheery weather report. Two days of clear, unseasonably cool weather.

Great, thought Merrit. Should be a real nice weekend.

It wasn't long before Noah let his eyelids close, and he drifted away from the noisy world of cartoons. Julie felt his brow. Noting no change, she pulled his special blanket away from him to keep him cool.

She shut the TV off, interrupting an on-screen explosion, and considered for a moment whether she wanted to lie down.

A few minutes, with her feet up, she thought. That

would be nice.

But she'd feel wasted afterwards, she knew; naps just sapped her energy for the rest of the day. She decided to go down to the basement and do some clay work. Something to take her mind off things.

The basement had a still-life quality. She hadn't been down there to work for over a week, and already her small studio had an abandoned look to it, with patches of dry clay forming crumbly islands on her table and a thin layer of dust lying on her unglazed pieces on the nearby shelves.

No matter, Julie thought. As soon as she started work everything would feel fine.

She dug out a good-sized chunk of moist gray clay from a thirty-gallon can she kept near her table. She plopped it on the center of the table, where its random form caught the overhead light like a craggy meteor.

Nothing useful today, Julie thought. No fancy bowls, or earthy goblets, or anything with a purpose. She'd just let her hands work the clay and let whatever happens happen.

She dug her fingers into the clay, and began the soothing process of alternately squeezing and rolling it, forcing out any hidden air bubbles. This was, in some ways, the best part. Mindless work really, yet its rhythmic movements relaxed Julie, and let her think.

Squeeze and roll.

While she worked, she catalogued her fears.

Noah. God, how she loved him. Not just because he was the youngest of her two. Sarah seemed to have been born with all the survival skills she'd ever need on this planet. She had it all: personality, looks, intelligence, guts.

But Noah was always a few degrees off. If it could go wrong, Noah would eventually stumble into it, provoking tears and, sometimes, Julie's anger. And while he was bright (able to name any dinosaur in a single glance), there were signs that a normal educational system might leave Noah tracked into a host of grisly "special classes."

Most of all, Noah radiated vulnerability. Not a day went by, Julie thought, that she didn't worry about some aspect of Noah's life. When he got sick, it devastated her.

Squeeze and roll.

Then there was her affair with Caldwell. Here she allowed herself a sick little grin. Who'd believe it? she often asked herself. Julie Riley had it all. A great, caring husband (and no Sunday football!), nice, healthy kids, and her own fledgling career.

All put in jeopardy—for what?

Fun. Maybe a little danger. If there's one thing she couldn't stand, it was boredom. And now she had risked it all.

Now she just hoped that she would escape, with no strings, and no great revelations. This isn't a movie, she told herself. It's over, and I don't have to get caught. I could run back to the safety of my family and never think about it again.

Yet, somehow, she felt it wasn't going to be that easy.

Squeeze and roll.

Then there was this other thing, all these missing people. It reminded her of the hot summer days when the Son of Sam was on the prowl. Before he was

194

caught, the Son of Sam would appear anywhere, shooting young women from Queens to the Bronx. He seemed virtually uncatchable, an evil phantom who came to own the city. One of Julie's friends, a teacher at Mount St. Vincent College, lived in Riverdale and would call Julie "just to talk." But Julie sensed her friend was afraid to even run out to the store for a container of milk.

Now, sleepy old Harley had its own maniac, specializing in just this one town, and accepting applications from victims of all ages.

Squeeze and . . .

There, she thought, leaving behind her unpleasant meditation. The clay is ready. She started shaping it, feeling for the form that she'd unleash. In her mind, she always felt that there was something in the clay, some shape ready to appear, and her hands merely served to help that process. Perhaps the clay, dug in this case from the hills of Virginia, carried some memory of a primeval earth, with massive volcanoes dotting the planet and new mountain ranges thrusting upward.

She took one part of the clay and shaped it, forming a graceful curve extending out. Then, just letting her hands roam over the clay, she pushed and smoothed some sections, until it almost resembled . . .

Julie laughed. Resembled nothing, she thought. Except maybe a wingless, headless goose.

The surface of the clay was drying. She went to the sink and filled an old potato-salad container with water. She paused near the stairs to listen for any sound of Noah. Nothing. She returned to the table.

195

It looked different. Her clay. It was—different.

She placed the water down beside her clay, and stared at it.

It seemed to have a head. The curved piece ended in a bulbous knob. It was ugly, thought Julie, disturbing. And she wondered. . . .

Did I make that?

She was sure she'd let the curve end, just end. After all, she wasn't out to make some kind of deformed duck decoy.

"Quack," she said aloud, her voice sounding hollow in the gloomy basement.

Well, I can always change it, she thought. That's the best thing about clay. If you don't like it, just crumble it into a ball and try it again. And this time she thought, she'd better pay attention to what she was doing so that she didn't end up with another weird animal.

She wet her hands and attacked the clay again, pulling at it, shaping it, sprinkling it with water to make it more malleable.

She stepped back.

It was the same thing. Same squat body and snake-like neck, peering out at the basement. And yes, she saw, it had a head again.

What the hell is it? she asked herself, feeling cold now.

She went to it, to wreck it again, to give up clay work for today.

But instead she looked at it, looked at what must be its feet flapping down from its side, and then the barrel-shaped body where she had put the small impressions of . . .

What could they be? Scales? Fur?

And the neck, craning out so far that she was sure the clay would give way, breaking off and plopping down onto the table. But most of all, there was the head. A different shape now, with just a hint of eyes carved out of the clay and a broad, thin line made by her fingernail to indicate a mouth.

She touched it and felt its still moist surface, then pulled back in revulsion, knowing. . . .

I didn't make this.

She took a deep breath and destroyed it, squeezing the clay, crushing it through her fingers, returning it to its former meaningless shape.

Julie didn't bother to put the clay away. Let it dry like that, she said to herself. Let it become a big, useless block of dried clay.

She shut the light off above the table and left the basement.

Mrs. Phelan's boarding house was one of two places that transients stayed while in Harley. Transients, that is, not tourists.

Tourists, as Mrs. Phelan was fond of telling people, didn't come to Harley. Why should they? A sprawling Ramada Inn that opened a few years earlier soon metamorphosed into some kind of resort, before finally ending up as an undernourished conference center.

The transients that Mrs. Phelan usually serviced in her sprawling, three-story home were most often people released from prison or visitors coming to see prisoners. She was usually the first stop on an ex-con's road back to somewhere. And she tried to make their few days with her as "homey" as possible. Her few rules—no guests, no noise, and no credit—were mixed with a generous supply of clean towels and a plain, hearty meal at dinner time.

Her latest guest was someone quite different. A real gentleman, she noticed. Polite, and well-dressed. From his accent, he came from Europe, maybe Germany or Austria. And he was a doctor of some kind.

She liked this Dr. Singer even if she couldn't figure out what he was doing in her boarding house.

Shelly was effectively marshaling her parents to guarantee that the pool party started promptly at 4 p.m. without any hitches.

She had her father make an early call to Al Davis, the weekend pool manager, to confirm that the pavilion, a garish, tent-like structure with a yellow awning, was indeed reserved. Then, she had her father check with the caterer who was to supply a ten-foot wedge, assorted cakes and munchies, as well as a cooler full of Coke in all its many guises—diet, new, cherry, caffeine-free, and, of course, classic.

It would be cool by tonight, Shelly knew, but that would give everyone a chance to put on some snazzy sweaters. And the music would just have to keep everyone moving.

No question about it, Shelly thought, it was simply going to be the best party yet.

*   *   *

James Baker slept late on Saturday, tuning out the sounds of his infant son, who seemed to spend all his waking hours crying. Baker eventually got up around ten and, after slugging some Tropicana OJ straight from the container, decided to call Mulcahy. When he didn't show up at the Tarrytown entrance point, Baker hadn't been too worried. He had certainly drunk a lot. But it wouldn't hurt to check up on how he did.

He dialed Mulcahy's number and his wife answered. Baker introduced himself and asked to speak to her husband.

But he wasn't there, he was told. Not to worry, though, she said. He often overdid it on a Friday night, ending the evening sleeping it off on some friend's couch. He usually showed up in the afternoon, she said. Just in time for a nap, she added laughing.

Okay, said Baker. And he hung up.

He walked into the kitchen, opened the refrigerator, and examined the foil-wrapped leftovers scattered on the shelves.

"Please take a seat, Captain."

The warden pointed to a sturdy, leather-backed chair facing his pristine desk top. Merrit admired Grossbach's blue suit—no off-the-rack job here. Warden business must be good. He also glanced at the wall filled with various diplomas and citations. A small family portrait seemed hopelessly outnumbered. The blinds behind the warden were open, and the main prison courtyard, now empty, was visible.

"I've gathered the files that should be of interest to you. There's only six that seemed appropriate. All released within the past two months. Most are repeat offenders, assorted felonies, grand larceny, the usual. There's only one murder-two conviction in the lot."

"I appreciate this, Mr. Grossbach," Merrit said leaning over to pick up the manila folders. He flipped through them quickly, looking at the mug shots and conviction records. He came to the last one. "This one looks like a handful," Merrit said holding the last folder open.

"We calmed him down. They all settle down here, Captain. We run a tight ship, and the sooner the inmates learn that the sooner they start enjoying life again."

"Eddie Dixon settled down, eh?"

Grossbach smiled. "Some take longer than others, but they all eventually adjust to the way we do things."

Merrit nodded, skimming through the folders a second time. "No rapes, no molestations, nothing that would seem to help us. Do you keep track of where they go when released?"

"Sure do. Most head back to whatever garden spot of the world they crawled in from."

"Any of them stay in town?" Merrit asked.

"Yes," the warden answered slowly. "Eddie Dixon. I wrote down his address and clipped it inside his folder. . . ."

"Good thing he's all calmed down," Merrit said. He stood up and shook Grossbach's hand. "Thanks for your help."

"Anytime."

Merrit left the prison and, with only a few wrong turns, found Eddie Dixon's current residence of record. He looked at the small, neatly painted sign hanging from a post. Mrs. Phelan's Boarding House.

He walked in and found a gray-haired woman knitting in a large chair while a German shepherd slept by her side.

"Mrs. Phelan?" Merrit said quietly. The woman looked over the edge of her bifocals. Merrit flashed his badge. "I'm a police captain, ma'am, and I'd like to speak to Eddie Dixon."

"Well," she said returning to her knits and purls, "you won't find him here. He hasn't been here since Thursday. Thursday morning, as a matter of fact."

Merrit stepped closer to her. The dog raised his blackish snout and opened his egg-shaped eyes. Doesn't miss a move, Merrit thought. "Could I see his room?" And please, lady, Merrit prayed. Don't make me waste my morning fetching a warrant.

"Guess so. Long as you leave everything nice and tidy. Mr. Dixon may be back. He's paid up till Sunday."

She got up with a loud sigh, the overstuffed chair seemingly unwilling to release her. For every two steps she took, the dog, keeping pace, took four.

"Now, quietly if you please, Captain," she said as she was about to go up the stairs. "Many of my gentlemen work at night and they need their sleep."

"Yes, ma'am," Merrit answered sharply. No funny business in the house, that's for sure.

She opened the door to a small room, just next to the second-floor landing. A single bed and a night table were the dominant pieces of furniture. A hard-backed chair with a red-leatherette seat was pushed flush up to a small table. A chest of drawers—child's furniture, really—was under the window. Except for a nearly empty bottle of Jim Beam on the table, there was nothing else visible.

Merrit opened the drawers and saw the truncated wardrobe of an ex-con. A few pairs of socks, a change of pants. Some boxer shorts and a white shirt. And nothing else.

He opened the drawer to the night table. There was a wallet with forty dollars, a Social Security card, and an aging picture of a young black woman.

"Gone since Thursday, eh?" Merrit said. "Any idea where?" Mrs. Phelan shook her head. No, he thought, she wouldn't be one to pry. "Thank you for your help," he said with a warm smile. Mrs. Phelan nodded and followed him to the door. He walked out to his car, wondering. . . .

Where is our friend Eddie Dixon? Did he just decide to take off somewhere? And though it hadn't been made public yet, where was Tommy Burdick's mother?

And just what the hell is going on in this town?

He was done. A neat stack of file cards before him. Jack leaned back in his uncomfortable chair, stretched, and rubbed his eyes. He looked at his watch. Merrit was due in fifteen minutes.

He looked over the two dozen names, nearly all of them unfamiliar. O'Keefe. Myers. Stein. Babcock. Stone. Kliber. Perez. Edelman.

Just names. People move out, and new people

move in. Kids are born, grow up to play on the cracked sidewalk, and then trace their initials in the wet cement when it's repaired. Then they're gone, lost to cars, college, and kids of their own.

He looked at his cards while waiting, noting the addresses, trying to see where people lived in relation to him.

Then he saw it.

A coincidence really, just one of those unusual things that happen, he guessed. Four names, four families, all buying their houses on the same block, the same year, and right next to each other almost. Now that's unusual, he thought. Sure it's a nice block. But not *that* nice. And how could four families decide to sell at the same time? Now that's really peculiar.

Why it's almost as if the families moved in together, like some kind of gypsies, or tribe of Indians, or . . .

He gathered the cards together for Merrit to take. At the last minute, he put the four houses on the same block on top. Make it easier for whatever cop checks them out.

The four from Schuyler Road.

What made Saturdays hard?

Ann Kenyon asked herself. It was the weekend, a time to relax and enjoy herself. A time away from the children at school. A time to spend with adults.

But it was none of that for her.

It was just time, time alone.

Years ago there'd been a few dates with respectable

boys, boys that her dad approved of. Most of the girls didn't wait for dates, they just sort of hung out on street corners, shooting the breeze. But her dad would have no part of it, not for his only little girl.

College was no better. Living at home and commuting to nearby Fordham didn't improve her social life, and her white girl friends at school didn't have a whole lot of guys to fix her up with.

She got up from the kitchen table and went to Mr. Coffee to refill her cup.

Maybe, she wondered, maybe if she hadn't had to take care of her father, maybe then she could have met someone. But when she wasn't trying to work hard in her first teaching job, she was home feeding her father mashed potatos and pureed meat. Day after day, with Momma long gone, she was his nurse and support. Her older brothers, with new families of their own, couldn't be bothered.

And she didn't complain.

After all, he had struggled to save enough to send her to a good school. And my, wasn't he so proud of her good grades, and wasn't he beside himself when the letter came informing her that she had a job.

Imagine, he would say laughing, my little Annie a teacher.

And now the apartment was hers. Somehow she had just never gotten around to moving. It still carried ghosts of her parents' life together. Family pictures in the living room, and a box of children's clothes in the closet, sealed up with tape for the grandchildren to wear. Clothes, she knew, that no one would ever wear.

She started back to the table with the cup of coffee. Her hand started to shake.

Slowly at first, then more violently until she grabbed it with her free hand, as her coffee sloshed over the side onto the gleaming white linoleum floor.

"No," she whispered to herself.

"No more." But the shaking spread through her body. She let the near-empty cup fall, and she aimed her shaking, collapsing body onto one of the chairs.

She sat there, then, shaking.

It was to happen again, she knew. The visit, the small talk, the serious looks, and then the clothes brought out of a Grand Union bag. She'd touch them.

Please. No.

She'd touch them. And then there'd be the pictures in her mind.

The horrible pictures. No one should have to see them. No one.

The shaking was stopping.

The phone rang.

PART III

Chapter 15

Shelly was cultivating a major pout, a full-scale, all-stops-out attempt to make her parents stop wrecking her party. Peter Jaffe, her father, feigned unconcern as he presided over a small bar and fixed drinks for whatever poolside friends came by to say hello. Shelly's goal was quite simple.

She wanted them to move to some other area of the pool before she died of embarrassment.

Jaffe's wife came up to him, treading gently, as she knew she must. She was dealing with the unusual configuration of her husband's two-martini consciousness. Logic, while not totally lost as in his three-martini condition, was, nonetheless, dangerously erratic.

"Peter," Susan Jaffe said touching a small point at the bottom of his elbow, "Shelly would like us to . . ."

"I know, I know. She wants us to get lost. But there's *going* to be adult supervision at this party," Jaffe said. "That's what we told all the parents. And that's what there will be. Now if Miss Sophisticated wants to pout away her whole party, fine." Jaffe looked over his wife's shoulder and saw Julie Reilly just entering the main gate with Sarah. He lost all interest in discussing things with his Rubenesque wife.

Susan backed away, embarrassed by her husband's obvious interest, and she went over to Shelly, who simply gave her the full, frozen impact of the sulk. As usual Susan Jaffe was caught in an impasse.

Julie stopped by Peter's bar as Sarah carried her bag over to Shelly.

"Hello, Peter. What are you running here, two parties?"

Peter gestured at the small, but well-stocked bar. "Oh, this? Just something to keep lingering parents gainfully employed. Could I interest you in, let's see, a vodka and tonic, if I remember correctly?"

"No, thanks. Maybe later, when I come to pick up . . ."

"With a lime twist, correct?" Peter said mixing the drink while Julie protested. "There. Sure, you can stay a moment. Enjoy watching the frolicking teeny-boppers." He grinned as he handed her the inviting drink.

Sarah, meanwhile, had crouched down to talk to Shelly.

"Damn parents," Shelly hissed. "I told them to go someplace else." She glanced at the food table where the boys were preying on the snacks. The wedge was safe for the moment, guarded by a big yellow cellophane wrapper. "And all the boys do is eat."

Sarah pulled off her Twisted Sister T-shirt and stepped out of her purple culottes. She caught one of the boys, Marty Kall, sneaking a look at her. Good she thought, smiling to herself. She enjoyed being noticed.

"Anyone go in the water yet?" she asked.

"No," Shelly grunted. "It's too cold."

"Well, c'mon," Sarah said, adjusting the tight elastic of her swimsuit bottom. "Let's go in and inspire everyone." She put her hands down to haul her friend up.

Shelly smiled, pulled herself up, and, with a departing scowl at her father, announced, "Last one in the pool cleans up." The boys, grinning and nudging each other, slowly followed the girls in.

"Ah, there they go," Peter said. "Great age, huh? No problems, nothing to worry about except getting your homework done. Your drink okay?"

Julie nodded. It was always strange to see Sarah with her friends, to see the kind of strength she seemed to have. Charisma, she guessed. She watched Sarah now, swimming with Shelly and Christina, pushing back her wet hair while the boys, still very much boys, looked at her dumbstruck. She was growing up and it scared her sometimes. Julie took a deep sip of her drink.

"Another? The evening is young." Jaffe reached for her glass.

"Oh, no. I've got a sick boy at home and Jack's waiting for me."

Peter leaned closer. "Well, you're always welcome for a drink in my house." He put a hand on her shoulder. "Anytime."

Julie stepped away. She looked at Jaffe's wife, puttering about the food table, knowing, Julie thought, exactly what kind of lech her husband was.

211

But then, who was she to question someone else's marriage? Julie thought sadly.

Susan Jaffe walked over timidly. "Hi, Julie. I hope there's enough food. I don't know how much the boys will eat."

"Same amount as the girls, but they eat six times a day," Jaffe laughed.

Julie smiled politely. "I gotta go. I'll be back in three hours." Then, looking right at Susan, "Hang in there."

Susan Jaffe watched Julie walk away, admiring her sleek poise, as she painfully noticed her husband watch Julie.

The high-pitched squeals of the girls caught her attention.

Christina Wilson was trying to dunk the cute blond boy, Steven Parker. Christina laughed and fought with a mock ferocity as she tried to push Steven's head under the water. Shelly was giggling at them, now letting her party roll along, tuning out her parents. She saw Patty Myers arrive, and she saw Mr. Myers stop by her father's impromptu oasis. Patty cautiously took off her street clothes and hesitantly entered the pool.

"Hey, Patty-cakes. About time!" Shelly yelled. Then she turned to the other girls and whispered something. She waited until Patty had entered the chilly water.

"Okay, now!" All the girls jumped up and swooped down on Patty, splashing her with waves of cold water. The boys looked on, wrestling with each other, diving off the side, sleek otters that circled the young girls with an eager anticipation of the year to come.

By the time the sun was sitting on the horizon, everyone had decided that they'd had enough of the pool. Shelly's mom came to her and quietly asked if it might be time to unwrap the wedge. The small but powerful TEAC speakers that Peter had hung from the poles of the pavilion were blasting a song called "Bad Boy." Christina and Sarah were dancing together as they sang, "Bad, bad, bad, bad boy, you make me feel so good." Shelly smiled, pleased with her party.

"Sure, Mom. Unwrap the wedge." Her mother nodded, happy to have something to do. Her husband was now playing host to the evening wind, hoisting a bottoms-up to the setting sun.

"Damn," Shelly said, looking at him. She walked over to the dancers, wiggling her body with moves picked up in her Advanced Jazz class at the Westchester Dance Conservatory. "Bad, bad, bad, bad boy!" she started to sing.

The wind picked up, cool, filled with the threat of a summer ending too soon. The party lanterns were plugged in as the sky turned from royal blue to a rich purple. The pool was nearly empty, except for a few hearty swimmers doing serious laps in the brightly lit water.

Al Davis, pool manager, walked over to Jaffe's bar. "Everything okay, Mr. Jaffe?"

Jaffe grinned, his airplane fuel kicking in nicely. "Fine, Al. Thanks," he said, fiddling in the pocket of his pool jacket for an envelope. "Here, for your help." He handed Al the envelope with three crisp ten-dollar bills inside. Jaffe congratulated himself. A real class act, he thought.

"Drink, Al?"

Al shook his head while he smoothly placed the envelope in his back pocket. "No, thank you very much, Mr. Jaffe. But I've still got a lot of work to do."

Right, thought Jaffe, like porking all the greased-up housewives who parade in front of you every damn day.

"Some other time, then," Jaffe said.

It was night.

Sarah's slice of the monster wedge had lost its greasy innards to the safety zone of the plate. While the bread was good, crispy and fresh, the salami and stuff was too oily for her taste. The boys, though, seemed to be eating it with gusto. Shelly stood next to Sarah.

"Brainstorm, Reilly. An authentic brainstorm. It's dangerous, but definitely worth it. Wanna hear it?"

Sarah zipped up her sweatshirt. It was getting really cool, she thought. "I'm all ears, Shelly."

Shelly pointed a finger right at her friend. "You, my dear, shall come to the sleep-over."

"I can't. You know that. . . ."

Shelly held up her hand. "Quietly, S.R., or you'll blow the whole caper. You go home. Go to bed. Then, after an hour or so, you sneak out to my house and the sleep-over. It's only about a block away. We just make sure you get back before sunrise. Just like a vampire. What do you say?"

Sarah shook her head. She at once felt oddly thrilled and then scared by the idea. "No. I wouldn' sneak out on my parents. Especially with some nu case running around."

214

Shelly put an arm around her friend, and pulled off to the side, out of the pavilion. "One block. That's all Sarah. For an hour, S.R. One hour. I'll even walk you back to your house."

"But what about your parents?"

"Them? Forget it. My father will be flat on his back before I get in the door. And my mom will have the TV blasting in her room so she won't hear us."

Sarah was still shaking her head.

Shelly looked her right in the eye. "Tell me that you'll think about it, S.R. Just think about it, okay?"

Sarah smiled and nodded. "Okay, okay," she said in her best valley-girl voice. "Hey, I'm going to change," she said. "It's too cold out here with just a sweatshirt on."

"Sure enough," Shelly said. "Me, I'm going to eat and talk to the boys."

Sarah picked up her straw bag, decorated with a garish woven butterfly of orange, blue, and green, and walked to the women's locker room. She entered and smelled the tangy odor of wet bathing suits and hot showers. The concrete floor was still brown with wetness, and the bare light bulbs gave the rows of lockers a forlorn look.

It's usually so crowded and noisy, thought Sarah. People excusing themselves as they stepped past someone's open locker, dodging a lady's over-padded behind. Then the sporadic slam of the lockers. Bang, bang. Then, a few beats later, another bang.

Now, it was just quiet.

She went to the locker and worked the combination. Her fingers slipped and she missed the last number. She had started again when . . .

She heard something.

One of the girls most likely, she thought. The night was turning cold, nasty. She was glad that she'd brought a terry-cloth outfit that, with her sweatshirt, should keep her plenty warm.

"Hey," she shouted. "Who is it? Shelly? Chris? Come over here."

No one answered as Sarah peeled off her tight black and orange swimsuit, slowly, craning her neck to hear . . .

No sound.

She shrugged, and reached into the bag to pull out her panties, shorts, and shirt.

She heard a footstep.

And, all of a sudden, she felt a million miles from the party. She was someplace else, somewhere that no one would ever hear her—

She stepped into her shorts quickly without bothering about the panties. Then the top. Faster, faster. But each hurried movement of hers only seemed to bring another step. Step. Step.

Until he was there. She stood still for a moment like a startled deer. Not moving, hoping the hunter would somehow lose sight of her amidst the brambles and leaves.

And then she seemed to hear him talk.

Hello, he seemed to say. Her lips parted and she said—

"Th-this is the women's room." She felt silly then. Of course, it's the women's locker room. Of course he knew that. That was just a silly thing to say. Why anyone could see that he knew where he was. He knew.

He stepped closer. She backed away.

She didn't back away.

Nothing happened. Her eyes began to fill with tears, slowly building, trickling down her cheek, oh-so-slowly, as she said, "Please. Please go away."

The man smiled. His eyes scanned her now, up and down, and she felt herself open to him completely, until it was as if she was naked and he was running his fingers across her, touching her, testing her.

He was next to her, so close his breath warmed her forehead. She looked at him, then she felt her fear ebb with every second he stood there. She became calm, and her breathing slowed. It was okay, this tall man standing close to her like this. She liked it, her mind suggested.

He touched her. His fingertips to her skull.

"Ohhh!" she howled. She screamed. Then it came to her. Complete, whole, everything.

She saw them all, inside his mind, at the very moment of their last horrible agony. She felt what they felt, and then went on to feel still more, until her body shivered like a pane of glass about to shatter. Good, he seemed to say.

He leaned forward to kiss her.

"Hey, Sarah, what are you doing in here?" From miles away Shelly's voice entered her mind, and then the man stepped back. Now she heard Christina. "Reilly, you got your own party going on here?"

They ran down the aisles to Sarah, but they stopped when they saw her. She was mumbling, crying to the air, her fists clenched tight. Shelly stepped close to her and raised a hand to her shoulder.

"No!" Sarah screamed. "No!" She flailed her fists, hitting Shelly on the forehead. Shelly turned to Christina and said, "Get my mom, quick!"

Shelly tried to hold her best friend close as Sarah's fists came down on her, harder and harder, and Sarah wailed, her voice echoing in the empty locker room. A single word over and over until it was just a hoarse whisper.

"No . . ."

Chapter 16

Sarah's dad was there in minutes, followed shortly by the police. They all asked her questions.

What had happened? Who was it?

And then, the hard one.

Where did he go, Sarah? Where is the man?

She tried to answer, she really did. But her answers left Chief DeFalco biting his lip and shaking his head. Her father went to Shelly and Christina for answers, which did no good at all.

Finally, Jack said he just wanted to get her home and into bed. He asked Tom DeFalco to see that someone was watching his home tonight.

"Not the neighborhood or the block, Tom. My house," Jack said, gritting his teeth. DeFalco nodded.

"Sure, Jack. I'll have Alan Smith there before you get home. Right outside the house."

Jack seemed to relax a bit. Without a word to the wobbly Peter Jaffe, he walked Sarah to the car.

On the way home he tried asking Sarah a couple of questions. But she started crying, a great, helpless shaking that had Jack gripping the steering wheel and praying to God that somehow he'd meet whoever it was that had done this to her.

Officer Smith was already in front of his house, lights out, radio on, when Reilly pulled into the driveway.

"Weird. Just too weird." Shelly looked right at Christina. "I mean, did you see anybody? No, of course not. And neither did I. You know, Sarah's a great kid but, hey, she really spooks me sometimes."

"Maybe," a small voice suggested, "maybe she's special."

"Special how, Patty?" Shelly asked with a trace of sarcasm in her voice.

"I read a book once. It was for a project. Some people can see things. Things that are there but not like, well, not really there."

"Like ghosts?" asked Christina laughing. "The Ghost of Harley Pool strikes again?"

"No," said Patty, her voice growing surprisingly strong. "There's some kind of force or something that moves around. Sarah's different. Maybe, maybe . . ."

"Maybe she's nutsoid!" laughed Shelly. She saw her mom waving from the pool entrance. "Hey, let's go. The car's out front."

They picked up their assorted bags and cases, leaving the still-lit party lanterns and Peter's disheveled bar behind, for the morning and Al Davis to handle. Susan Jaffe had tried to cancel the sleep-over after the "disturbance" as she called it. But Shelly had flared up, and her mother had quickly backed down.

What, after all, had happened? Shelly had asked. Sarah Reilly saw someone. Or *thought* she saw someone in the women's lockers. And she freaked out.

Big. Deal.

The sleep-over, Shelly had informed her parents, was on. Christina, Patty, Sharon, and Shelly jumped into the back of the Chrysler station wagon.

And off they went.

"Watch this!" Shelly squealed, a redundant directive since everyone's eyes were glued to the screen. "He actually gets up again!" The girls watched the prone figure of Jason, decorated with multiple stabbings and hatchet wounds, start to move. His hockey mask made him look like the goalie of gore. And then he popped up like some crazed wind-up doll. On cue, the girls screamed. "Can you believe it?" laughed Shelly.

"How do they kill him?" Sharon asked, trying to sound casual.

Shelly grinned malevolently. "They don't. Not in this movie, anyway. There's two more sequels after this one before he's finally dead."

"If then," Christina said sardonically. "You know, I can't believe that your parents let you rent this yucky stuff."

"And I can't believe that they gave you your own VCR," Sharon added.

221

"It just because they love me so much," Shelly sighed, blinking her eyes.

"Hey," Sharon squawked, scrounging around the bottom of the potato chip bag, "no more chipos!"

"No more chips *here*," Shelly corrected her. "I'll be right back, and I'll get more soda too." She got up to leave.

"Aren't we ever going to sleep tonight?" Patty asked no one in particular.

"What's the matter?" Christina said, tossing a pillow at Patty. "Surely you know that that's the one thing you *don't* do at a sleep-over."

"Right," Shelly said, opening her door, "and keep the screaming down till I get back, okay?"

She walked down the dark hall past her mother's room, where she heard the muffled gabbing of some late-night talk show. Looking down the staircase, she saw the light that spilled from the kitchen into the first-floor hallway.

She heard a heavy thump over her head, probably one of her friends rolling off the bed, she thought. She walked into the kitchen, large and spacious, gleaming with modern, well-cleaned appliances. She opened the cupboard nearest the refrigerator and saw a bag of Wise Potato Chips, the last one, flanked by boxes of spaghetti and cans of Chicken of the Sea tuna. She grabbed the bag and tossed it onto the kitchen table. Then she opened the portals to the magic kingdom of the fridge.

"Damn," she said searching the suddenly barren lower section.

The soda was all gone. No big problem, though.

She'd just have to go down to the small shelves that lined the basement stairs. There'd be lots of soda there—warm, of course. She made a mental note to bring some ice upstairs.

She opened the door to the basement. There was enough light for her to see and grab a six-pack each of Cherry Coke and 7-Up. She turned to go back in the kitchen.

The light went out.

Shelly stopped for a minute, her pulse quickening. Then she stepped into the kitchen, half-expecting to see one of her friends.

She heard a sound, turned, and saw someone in the shadows. A man, dappled by slices of moonlight.

"Dad?" she said quietly. "Is that you? I'm trying to . . ." She paused. "Dad?"

No, it's not, she seemed to hear.

Then, with a hint of amusement, she heard the man say slowly, quietly—

"I'm not Dad."

There's something soothing about making bread, thought Eleanor Cowles. It filled the spare hours while one waited for something. It was warm, nourishing, and comforting when you were up late at night, when the street sounds had all faded away.

Of course, it was just a habit from her teenage years, learned from her father as he took her from one distant location to another. From the boggy fens of Norway to the sweaty jungles of the Yucatan, it was somehow a constant, providing a thread of normalcy, something to keep her rooted in the here and now.

She opened the oven, its blurry, fat-splattered window all but useless. The old electric oven had proven to be a reluctant baking partner.

The bread was a rich, crusty-topped golden brown, ready for some thick pats of butter. It smelled wonderful.

The phone rang. She picked it up urgently, listening, her mouth nervously nibbling her lower lip. She nodded to herself, and then said, "Yes." She hung up.

Eleanor Cowles slipped the bread out of the oven, letting it sit on top, and clicked the oven off. Hurrying now, her fingers nervously worked the strings of her apron. She left the house lights on, and went out her back door, out across the street.

She walked around to the side of the big white house, to Kliber's house, moving faster as she neared the door. She opened it, and entered the basement.

Shelly's mouth was covered by a heavy plastic tape that muffled any sound she made. Each of her wrists was securely tied to the arm of the sturdy oak chair, which was screwed to the floor. More rope, covered with stains here and there, went around her chest, compressing her so tightly that her breaths were shallow, and the air hissed through her nostrils.

She watched the three men, the tall one the others called Kliber and the two younger ones who had tied her to the chair. Then a woman entered, with a round, smooth face that raised Shelly's hopes that maybe everything would be okay now.

Maybe the woman would tell them that it was all over. No more fun and games. Break it up, please. And like the bullies in school, they'd listen and move away.

But then she saw the woman's eyes and she lost all hope. They were the bright, unfeeling eyes of a stray cat in the night, or worse, some roadside animal merely glimpsed as your car sped away. The look just wasn't human.

Shelly's yell died in her gullet, but she twisted back and forth, ineffectually struggling, back and forth. She wouldn't allow herself to think about what they might do to her.

Kliber walked to a curtained wall and tugged on the heavy purple material, revealing a wondrously large mirror, strangely beveled at the edges. Shelly stopped struggling, examining the blurry mix of color and light that filled it.

The people started saying words, nonsense words, Shelly thought, or some strange, ancient language that she knew no one must speak anymore.

The gibberish terrified her more than the slowly clarifying image.

Kliber stepped close to the mirror, his hand shaking, while the others kneeled. They were mumbling the gibberish more quickly now, racing through some demented Kaddish. Spittle gathered at the corners of their mouths, but they didn't pause in their recitation. Kliber glanced at Shelly. Her head twitched now, repeatedly kicking back in a mute, frenzied scream. Kliber leaned over her, just as the mirror became clear. He kissed her forehead.

The others felt it. The sudden surge of energy that flowed into the room as the young girl's fear was allowed to build even higher, teased by the man's touch, so that she didn't see the thing in the mirror.

Not at first.

But then it was there, almost in the room, peering out with bulbous eyes that seemed eternally hungry. Kliber left Shelly and stepped closer to it. And now, he spoke.

"Ia," he whispered. Then again. "Ia." The creature looked down at him, then at the girl.

She shuddered. Convulsively.

It extended an arm out, through the mirror, into the room . . .

. . . through the mirror, until it hovered over her head. Its hand-thing opened and closed, and row upon row of tiny teeth glistened from inside its palm. It seemed to hesitate. Then it fell upon her, instantly, viciously, the room filling with tearing and slurping sounds as Shelly's swollen veins spurted her life all over the concrete floor.

Their crazed voices seemed like hundreds in the small room.

When it was done feasting, it turned to the man, its arm dripping, searching, still hungry, and the man reached out for it. "Ia," he whispered again. Kliber raised his hand slowly. They touched—the gentle, long-awaited caress.

And it was gone.

The mirror now only reflected back the dingy, stained walls and floors of the basement. Slowly, the others stood up, their blood-speckled faces transfixed with joy. Eleanor Cowles approached Kliber, tears in her eyes.

"Yes?" she asked.

Kliber nodded, and the two younger men came closer, excited, a bit awkward, because who wouldn't be—in the presence of a God.

They touched Kliber.

It was then, neighbors said the next morning, as they boarded their Voyagers and Volvos for their white-steepled churches, that they heard something. Some screaming on the street, or a car breaking down, or maybe some teenagers outside raising hell. It awoke them, but they would let the hum of the air conditioners lull them back to sleep.

They touched him, and Kliber began to change, his body melting into the creature, his head inflating like a flaccid, leathery balloon suddenly injected with air, while his arms popped and swelled and pulsated.

They backed away, their excitement dying in their suddenly dry throats. One of the men moaned. And Eleanor, for a moment, thought of her bread.

The creature breathed in their fear, just a moment, before touching them.

One claw-like hand went for Eleanor's intestines and ripped them out even as she struggled to back away. The other hand snapped over to one of the men, who was running to the door. It closed around his wind pipe and snapped shut. The head plopped dully to the hard floor.

But the third man got to face the creature's mouth, a vast shaft of unearthly drool that all his babbled words of worship did nothing to appease.

It moved invisibly, instantly, to eat a hole in the screaming man's chest.

It was hungry.

It would always be hungry. But never more than now. Never more than on this day.

And when all were eaten, it became the man again.

Chapter 17

In the middle of the night, Julie, still not asleep, reached out for Jack. She touched him, tentatively at first, but feeling him harden, she started a smooth, gentle rhythm, rubbing him. And when he was fully erect, and his mind pleasantly brought to the foggy edge of awareness, she deftly climbed on top of him, letting him enter her in one prolonged movement.

She moved up and down, her fingers straying to roughly twist her nipples, then down to press hard just above her vagina. Jack's eyes were now open, and he was plunged suddenly into the desperate demands of Julie's body.

His hands went to her hips, pulling her down even harder on him, and then he arched up to meet her.

She moaned, close to the edge now. Jack struggled to match her passion, though he felt as though he had suddenly stumbled upon a very wild party.

She came down hard, and ground her groin into his, twisting, trying to fuse their bodies together. "Oh . . . God," she whispered, her mind finally cleared of all thoughts except this one sensation of release.

Her nails dug into Jacks chest as she reached an orgasm. When she realized that Jack hadn't come, she started her movements again. Jack pulled her down to kiss her.

"Don't worry about it, babe. It takes hours for my libido to wake up. I'll save it for tomorrow night." He gently turned her to the side and slid out of her, kissing her again on the lips. "Go to sleep, Julie," he whispered.

"Forget it, Captain," Jack snapped, holding the door open but quite pointedly not inviting Merrit in. "You can't expect me to leave the house. Not today. I'd be crazy . . ."

"You'd be crazy not to." Merrit's face looked haggard, and his voice lacked its usual bantering air. "You'd be crazy to sit here and hope that it all just goes away." Merrit looked around, as if searching for inspiration. "Look what we have going on here. Please. Your whole town is crawling with police, we're checking on anyone with a record within a twenty-mile radius, and DeFalco and his people have started interviewing people new to Harley." Merrit sucked on his ever-present cigarette. "And whoever's doing it just doesn't give a shit. No, sir. Do you realize that Shelly Jaffe disappeared from her house, Jack? Her own house, for Christ's sake."

"And that's why I'm staying right here," Jack said, a trace of belligerence in his voice. He glanced back into the living room. Noah seemed oblivious to the conversation as he watched the USA Network's Sunday cartoon marathon. Sarah was still in her room, probably still crying. The first call about Shelly had come from Christina, around 5 a.m., and Sarah had been crying off and on since then.

Jack shook his head. "Since the town can't protect anyone, I'm staying here."

Merrit pointed at a blue-and-white Harley police car parked in front of the house. "There's your protection, Jack. Smith has gone home, and now Officer Barron is here. And he'll *stay* here every minute that you're with me."

"But this guy," Jack said, clenching his fists, spitting out the words, "this guy came after Sarah. Who's to say he won't do it again? And how can you ask me to leave?" Julie appeared at his side, and Jack put his arm around her.

"How can you not go? If I go alone, with just some clothes, well, we might find out something and we might not. But if you're there, if Ann Kenyon can talk to you, we might get just what we need. A face, maybe. And maybe, if we're lucky, a name. Jack . . . I just don't have the time to find someone who knew all the missing people." Jack was aware of Merrit's use of the word "knew." Merrit let his cigarette butt fall to the ground.

"You've got to do it."

A mocking bird chirped loudly from the wire and cables that ran across the street.

Jack looked at Julie, then he pointed at the police car. "He'll stay here all day?" he asked Merrit.

"Until you tell him to leave."

"What do you think, Julie?"

Julie tried to be strong. All she wanted was to shut the door, slam it even, forget Merrit. But she thought of the others, those who now spent their days wondering just where someone they loved might be. Were the someones still alive? Or had they been cut up into tiny little pieces and thrown in some foul-smelling pit somewhere? And by now everyone pretty well thought they knew the answer to that one.

And, she told herself, the police car would be just outside, nice and close, windows open, ready to hear anything. What could happen?

"Go," she said. "We won't budge, and Paul Barron is big enough to scare anyone away." She smiled weakly. Then, "Go, but get the hell back here as fast as you can."

"Shit," Jack muttered. He shook his head at Merrit. "Wait a minute and I'll get dressed."

As Jack got ready, Merrit tried to relax. He knew it could really help having Jack along; maybe it was even crucial. He lit another cigarette, giving himself over to the chain-smoking that would possess him until the case was finished, one way or the other.

He loosened his tie. Nine a.m., and it was real hot already, and it was supposed to be a record-breaking scorcher by this afternoon.

James Baker's wife shook her husband awake. He turned from her, pulling a pillow over his head.

"There's a phone call!" she bellowed at him. "The lady says it's important, about your friend Mulcahy."

Slowly, Baker let his head emerge from his foam-rubber carapace. "What does she want?" he grunted.

"*I* don't know," his wife sang airily, walking away. "But she was crying on the phone."

Baker kicked his sheet off, got up, and walked bare-assed into the kitchen. He padded past his son, who was bombing the linoleum with dollops of oatmeal. Baker stood on top of one salvo and picked up the phone off the kitchen table.

"Hello," he said. He listened, blinking awake, as Mulcahy's wife told him that her husband had never come back, and that he'd never been away this long, *never*, and would Baker know anything at all about where he might be?

And Baker thought of the aqueduct, and the webbing, and drunken old Mulcahy stumbling around with a lit acetylene torch. Then he flashed on a picture of Mulcahy face down in three inches of slimy water, choking his life away.

"I dunno," he said. "But look, Mrs. Mulcahy, I know where he was going on Friday afternoon, and I'll call the police and tell them." Her crying made him pull the earpiece away. "And maybe," he said, "maybe I'll see if I can find him."

Baker accepted her bleary thank-you's and pressed the disconnect button on the cheap touch-tone phone. Then he called the police.

"Who are you calling?" his wife asked.

But Baker just held up his hand.

"Hello, police? I'd like to report a missing person. Yeah, a man who's missing." Baker paused. "And I think I know where he might be."

DeFalco was questioning people in Harley when he heard his police radio hiss for his attention.

"Chief," Sergeant Ralson said, "a Mrs. Gorman

just called in. Says that her husband and some of his buddies are holding some kind of vigilante meeting in his basement. She says they've got guns and beer—"

"They're still there?" DeFalco interrupted.

"When she called they were. She sounded pretty scared. Should I send a car ove there?"

That would be just the wrong thing to do, Falco knew. A few brash cops could set off a powder keg like that without even thinking about it. "No. I'll check it out. What's the address?"

DeFalco scribbled down the information.

He hurried to the house, a split-level ranch with a gaggle of four-by-fours and small vans outside.

He parked his car and walked quickly to the door. He rang the bell, and was let in by a small woman with mousy brown hair.

"Thanks for calling," DeFalco said quickly. "Are they downstairs?"

The woman nodded. DeFalco could see that she was scared. He heard the sound of the men echoing up from the basement.

As he walked down he was greeted by the stale smell of smoke and beer. The voices were loud. It could almost be a Sunday afternoon football game with the boys. That is, if it weren't for the Winchester hunting rifles and semi-automatics lying across their laps.

Jesus, thought DeFalco. Anything could happen down here.

"So . . . we'll divide up the town," one of the men was saying.

Another one of the men heard DeFalco's steps and

gradually they all turned and faced the Police Chief.

"Is this a private party?" the Chief asked in the sudden quiet. "Or can anyone with a gun join in?"

"The guns are all registered, Chief. And yes, this is a private party."

DeFalco took the remaining steps down, wishing that he was taller than his piddling five feet, eight inches. "Tom Gorman?" he asked looking at the man standing in front of him. The man nodded.

DeFalco looked around at the others. A few he recognized. Kevin Burns from Harley Hardware Store. Alex Scaputto, owner of a tow shop. There were others that DeFalco didn't recognize. And all around them, clusters of empty beer cans.

"We've got the right to assemble," Gorman said, and the other men grunted in agreement.

"So what are you going to do?" DeFalco asked quietly. "Patrol the streets, keep Harley safe, is that it, guys?"

"Someone's got to protect the town," Scaputto said snidely. "God knows you cops aren't doing such a good job." The men laughed.

"Right," Gorman said, raising his voice. "We've got homes, and wives, and kids, and someone's going around snatching people, doing who knows what kind of shit. Well, we're going to just give you police a hand. Ain't that right, fellows?"

There was a chorus of muttered assent.

DeFalco smiled. "Good," he said, eyeing Gorman's heavy-duty rifle. An M16, DeFalco knew. "'Cause we sure could use some sharp-witted vigilantes with quick reflexes. Why—"

And then DeFalco moved, smoothly, quickly. A

step towards Gorman, and his hand had closed around the gun barrel and effortlessly swung it out of Gorman's hand.

DeFalco had it pointed right at Gorman.

"Yeah," he continued. "Some really quick-witted help. It's just what we need."

DeFalco let the gun barrel swing around, making a casual survey of the room. "Some beer-bloated gun nuts walking around the town. You know," DeFalco said, raising his voice, "you guys would just end up making a lot more work for my police. Which is probably just what our maniac out there would love to see."

One of the men in the corner was putting his rifle back in its vinyl case. The sound of the zipper closing seemed to trigger a few others to start rooting around for their gun cases.

"You can't tell us not to protect the streets, DeFalco. We have every—"

"Yeah, I know," DeFalco grinned, "you got rights. And I got a town to protect. And if I think your presence is obstructing that job, I can throw your ass in jail." DeFalco took a step toward Gorman and looked him right in the face.

"And if you don't believe me, just give it a try." He looked around the den. "Now if the rest of you want to help, you'll get home, park your truck or van, and spend the weekend keeping your family safe and sound. Then at least we won't have to worry about you."

Gorman stood perfectly still looking down at the Chief. Then he backed away, his left hand searching for his beer. DeFalco heard other zippers, enough for him to know that, for today at least, the vigilantes wouldn't ride.

Checking that the safety was on, DeFalco threw Gorman's gun over to him.

"And, guys, don't make me interrupt my work again." DeFalco headed back up the stairs, followed sheepishly by some of the erstwhile vigilantes.

When he got back to his car he called his report in to Ralson. He told the sergeant he was going to head over to Schuyler Road, to talk to some newcomers to Harley. A quiet street. And probably, DeFalco sighed, another waste of his time.

When people talked about the changing "character" of New York, it was places like Fordham Road and the Bronx that came to mind. While the famous landmarks themselves were unchanged, like the Bronx Zoo, and the Botanical Gardens, and Fordham University, the universe around them had changed.

The old restaurants, like Murphy's Steak House, had given way to Burger Kings and Orange Julius. Random, mindless robberies and the riots from over a decade ago had brought about the heavy, corrugated steel doors that now covered all the shops at night, while bodegas and botanicas proudly displayed their wares on the same strip with Crazy Eddie.

Though the older people, the ones left behind, said that the neighborhood was gone, shot, down the tubes, anyone with eyes to see the children playing in the hydrants on the side streets and the laughing, colorful crowd walking past the shops knew that it was still a neighborhood.

"Hey," Merrit said looking out his window, "White Castle. I'll spring for lunch later."

"White Castle? What's that?" Jack asked disinterestedly, looking out at the squat little building that did, indeed, look like a white castle.

"White Castle. Just about the best hamburger ever invented. They're these little square burgers with holes in them, fried with onion and served on a tiny little bun. They used to be fifteen cents, and you could eat seven or eight at a sitting, no problem."

Jack shook his head. "Can't imagine getting that excited over a hamburger."

"Oh no? I've heard stories of Hollywood stars having them shipped out hot. Once you taste one, you're hooked for life."

Jack smiled. "If you say so." Merrit concentrated on driving through the crowded street. "We're almost at Ann's apartment."

Jack let the mental aroma of rows of White Castle hamburgers give way to the apprehension he felt. Going to a psychic seemed so off the wall. And if it wasn't for the fact that Merrit was so serious about it, Jack would be making goofy jokes.

Merrit turned down Prescott Street, stopping to let a spiffily dressed family of churchgoers cross. He found a parking space and pulled in.

"Lock it," he said to Jack. "Police radios have a habit of disappearing around here." Merrit snatched a shopping bag from the back seat.

They walked briskly, into a burnt-orange apartment building. Most of its windows were open to the hot morning air and the smell of exhaust. A few apartments had air conditioners tentatively balanced on the windowsills.

They walked up three flights, the stale odor of urine filling the darkened staircase. Somewhere a baby wailed. As they passed one door, angry voices screamed back and forth.

Merrit knocked at the door of Apartment 3-C. They heard the spy hole being flipped open. A moment later the door chain was removed, the dead bolt turned, and at last the door opened.

"Ann," Merrit said with genuine warmth, giving the petite woman a big hug. "How are you?" He casually placed the bag down just inside the door.

She gave Merrit a big grin and it was clear to Jack that she liked him immensely. "Not bad, Captain. Still teaching kids, still single, still looking."

"Oh," Merrit said, pointing over his shoulder, "this is Jack Reilly. He's here to, er, help." Jack smiled at Ann.

"I have coffee ready in the kitchen," she said, as if remembering her hostess duties. "And some fresh crumb cake."

"Good," Merrit laughed. "You always have something on hand to wreck my diet. Lead on."

In the small kitchen, Jack sat down facing a window that looked out on a building an arm's length away. Ann poured coffee, and set the crumb cake all neatly cut into squares in the center of the table.

For a while, as they sipped coffee and ate the deliciously spongy cake, they might have been on a nice Sunday visit. Jack listened while Ann told Merrit about her current class and how her brothers were getting on.

Finally, trying not to be abrupt, Merrit stood up. "I think that we'd better get started."

Ann nodded grimly, and put down her cup with a nervous click of porcelain. Jack felt as if he was attending a service of some unfamiliar faith, as Ann shut the lights off and pulled down the window shade, darkening the room to a closet-like gloom. Merrit brought in the bag he had dumped by the door.

When Ann sat down, she was shaking, Jack noticed. Tiny tremors that raced along her body, barely visible. Her breathing was uneven, labored, and her eyes darted left and right.

"Are you ready?" Merrit asked. Ann nodded. "If you have any questions, Jack knows the people. Okay, here we go."

The bag rustled as Merrit brought out a small blue-and-red striped shirt. It was speckled with yellow paint in a few places. Its odor, the slight tanginess of a small boy's sweat, wafted into the small kitchen. Gently, Merrit passed it over to Ann.

She groaned. "Oh . . . my . . . God," she said. And then she cried out. "Oh my sweet baby. He's gone," she said, looking up in astonishment to Merrit. Then more slowly, as if the image became clearer, "The boy is gone. It's . . ."

She hesitated, searching for the right word. A boom box blasted a rap song from the street below. "It's as if he's gone somewhere else, some other country. . . ."

(But those trees? Her mind asked. Where do you find such trees? Not here, not on this . . .)

240

Jack felt uncomfortable, and, to ease the feeling, he spoke.

"His name is . . ."

"Tommy," Ann said, laughing through her tears. "Always in trouble, such a headache to his mother. But a good boy, deep down, a sweet kid." She looked at Merrit, sorrowfully. "I don't know where he is. He's just . . . gone."

The bag rustled again. Merrit passed her a large, cotton-white blouse. It too had not been cleaned. "Oh," she said brightly, "what a *fine* woman. She loved to sing, oh yes. What a wonderful person to have—" she looked at Jack, "—as a friend. She never told you about her family, about losing them all. . . ."

Jack wanted it to stop. He wanted to get up and walk out of this kitchen. He was startled by Ann's voice.

"Wait a minute! Someone's grabbed her!" The muscles tightened in Ann's face, her lips pulled back in rage, in fear. Her hands twisted the cloth, knotting it, as she spoke through her clenched teeth. "Let-me-go," she screamed. "Let-me-go! Oh no, not Helen. Not this woman. She's stopped struggling, she's not fighting him. Why did she stop? Fight, Helen!" Ann pleaded. "Fight! Wait! There are other people. In a room."

Merrit raised his eyebrows.

"And there's a window. No, not a window, but some kind of mirror, and, and . . . and something in the mirror. Don't let it touch her, don't let it . . ."

She stood up. "No. No more," she cried. "No more people from your bag." As if punishing herself, she grabbed the bag from Merrit and dumped its contents on the table

A Harley High T-shirt and a pair of girl's shorts tumbled out. She put her hands down onto them, as if grabbing eels out of a bucket. "No! They're all gone. It's grabbed them up and taken them somewhere. And now there's just this, this man left. . . ."

She was shaking and screaming, her fists clenched tight against her chest. "Oh, sweet Jesus, you've got to stop him."

Jack reached out to her, not even hearing Merrit's warning yell, reached out to hold her, to somehow pull her close and end the horror that filled her. At the moment his hands went to her shoulders, her eyes turned to him, wide with terror, and Ann Kenyon spoke the words that Jack would hear the rest of his life. Words said slowly, quietly, with the utter resignation of hopelessness.

"He's. At. Your. House. *Now*."

She dissolved in tears.

Two flights down, a baby began to cry.

Chapter 18

From time to time, when a commercial didn't snare his interest quickly enough, Noah would slide off his perch on the couch, walk to the window, and look at the policeman waiting just outside his house.

His mother had told him that the police car would be staying there all day, right in front, but it's there to watch over the whole neighborhood. Everybody.

But why, Noah asked, why is he in front of *our* house?

His mother simply answered, "I don't know," and found some urgently invented task awaiting her in the kitchen.

Noah could hear the crackle of the police radio. He saw the policeman speak into it, just like on TV. He saw him wipe his brow. And then he saw him cranking the window shut.

Noah went back to his cartoons.

DeFalco looked at the mirror.

And thought . . . crazy place for a mirror. Unless, of course, the owner likes to give kinky New-York style parties in his basement, complete with leather masks and chains and . . .

He didn't see the spots on the floor, not at first. The light was sort of washed-out, diffuse, and the stone slab floor just looked like an ordinary basement floor. Just another dank basement.

Then he noticed the discoloration at his feet. He crouched down and put his fingers to the various red stains, overlapping each other. Maybe I should call up some help, he thought. Maybe . . .

He was afraid.

He looked back at the mirror and saw a scared man looking back at him. It was his secret, he knew. And the only person who could tell was dead.

DeFalco had started out as a New York City cop. "Twenty years, in and out," the old-timers would say laughing. And then you could retire to Florida and start some sideline operation like insurance sales or security work.

It had sounded good to DeFalco. Except the city every now and then liked to eat a cop, usually some good-looking cop with a wife and three kids. Then the mayor and an honor guard of bigwigs would see the victim off to an early grave.

DeFalco had been more nervous about that than he could ever admit. He liked police work, cruising the streets in one of the big old Chrysler patrol cars. But getting shot at. Well, that was something else.

DeFalco looked at the mirror, and once again he was there.

He and his partner, an older and experienced cop named Will Hanley, got a call—policeman in need of assistance—an expression which usually meant that some cop was in way over his head.

They sped to the location given, a dirty little side street amid the meat markets of the Lower West Side.

They got out of the car and walked over to find the cop sitting by his radio waiting for them. He told them that there was some kind of deal going on inside a warehouse directly across the street.

Hanley told the cop to watch the exit and then he rushed over to the warehouse, followed by DeFalco, who felt a chilly sense of unreality. It was like some kind of bad movie. We can't really be going in there to have a shootout with some hoods, he thought.

But Hanley ran in, his gun ready, telling DeFalco to stay right behind him. And DeFalco froze.

Hanley walked ahead, not even noticing DeFalco just wasn't there anymore. And the guy leaped out at Hanley, leaping just where DeFalco should have been watching Hanley's back, and it was all over for Hanley. Then the man with the knife turned, Hanley's blood still dripping from the knife, and he saw DeFalco standing in the shadows. And then he grinned, and darted away.

It was the grin that DeFalco would never forget.

Soon he left the New York City police force and made his way to Harley, a quiet town.

And now the face was in this mirror, DeFalco saw, looking right at him. That face, that sick smile. Over twenty years later, and it was coming for him now. He stepped backward and tripped, falling into a small chair, and DeFalco just couldn't move.

Outside, his radio kept calling over and over for him to answer.

Barron had debated closing the window. He had

been told to leave it open, plain and simple. But, hell, he could see the whole house clearly and it was too damn hot to just sit here and fry under the windshield.

He started the car and shut the window, rolling it up fast as he punched the AC-Max button. It spewed forth a burst of stale, warmish air. Barron waited for it to make the welcome shift to cool and then cold air. Like the six-liter, eight-cylinder engine, the Chrysler air conditioner was one powerful baby, reserved for heavy-duty vehicles.

In a few moments it was winter in July.

He looked at the house. A minute ago a little boy had popped his head under the blinds. Two blue eyes stared long and hard at him as if he couldn't be seen. Then he disappeared.

Barron glanced at the rear-view mirror, a bit of movement catching his eye. He saw someone about a block away. He craned his neck around to look through the back windshield and saw a man in a sky-gray suit walking on the Reillys' side of the block. It made Barron feel uncomfortable just to look at him. He wondered how anyone could wear a tie on a hot day like this.

Barron went back to looking at the rear-view mirror, noticing that the man's pace was steady. He almost seemed to be walking towards the police car. When he was abreast of the car door, he stopped and gently tapped at the window.

Barron looked up at the man. He wore the perplexed mask of someone timidly seeking help. Barron smiled at him, flipped the radio off, and rolled down the window.

The man's grin broadened.

For a split-second, Barron had an odd, anxious feeling that made his stomach muscles tighten.

"What can I . . ."

Then his mind began its roller-coaster plunge. As time slowed to a painful crawl, he watched the hand reach into the car. His own hand went up to catch it but, strangely, it just didn't move fast enough.

Then the man's hand became something else, as it settled on his head, as if he was being fitted for a skull cap. He felt the razor-sharp scratches of the rows of teeth ripping through his skull and a watery drool dripped onto his lips. He shrieked.

His head was covered completely, as if a lizard-skin ski cap was pulled down to his shoulders. Something snapped. Then the claw was gone, leaving behind the headless trunk of Paul Barron, rocking back and forth in the seat, shooting blood like a geyser straight up to the pale-blue roof of the car. Barron's arms danced spasmodically in the air.

Noah had seen it.

The tall man, he said to himself. He had seen the man's hand change into something else, like something from He-Man, or Dungeons and Dragons, and he knew he had only a very, very short time left. He locked the door, the way he saw his Daddy do it at night.

His small, bare feet padded up the stairs, pressing hard against the thick carpet, pumping his way upstairs, up to his sister.

To save her.

He burst into her room, breathless, yelling, hoping that for once she'd listen to him.

"Sarah . . . he's here. You've got to get out of here. He's coming to get you, Sarah."

Sarah turned toward her brother in surprise. *"Who's* coming for me?" she said slowly, her heart skipping a beat.

"The tall man. He's right outside."

Now Sarah grew stern.

"Noah! Stop trying to scare me. There's no one here. There's a police car outside, for Pete's sake."

Noah began to cry.

Just like my dream, he thought in panic. And he knew how that turned out.

"Please, Sarah? Please get away?"

"Okay, okay," Sarah said. It wouldn't hurt to take a look outside. "Just stop crying. I'll look out the bathroom window. You'll see, no one will be there."

Dressed only in a short nightie and panties, Sarah walked across the hall, to the bathroom, and a window that overlooked the street. Where she saw nothing.

"See?" she said smugly, looking up and down the block. "There's no one outside."

"Look in the *car*," Noah begged.

"Okay. I see . . ."

(I see a body without a head.)

She gagged.

It seemed forever before she could bring herself to turn, grab Noah's ice-cold hand, run down the stairs

Jack was at the apartment door fiddling with the

assorted locks, trying to open them and run out.

"God damn it," he yelled. "Open the door. And," turning to Merrit, "give me your car keys."

Ann Kenyon could barely walk, but she moved quickly to the locks.

"I'm calling DeFalco," Merrit said. "Barron's right there." He went to the phone and dialed. "Merrit here. Tell Barron to get inside the house now. And tell DeFalco to get over there. Move, Sergeant. We'll meet him there." He hung up. "Let's go."

Jack bolted out the door, taking steps two and three at a time while Merrit struggled to keep up with him.

Ann Kenyon leaned against the door and, sobbing uncontrollably, knew it was too late.

Noah stumbled, but Sarah held onto his arm, almost lifting him into the air to keep him from tumbling down the stairs. Even as he kicked his feet to get control of his careening body, he heard the solid click of the Yale lock popping open—a smooth, almost eager sound.

When they turned at the first-floor landing and started to cross the suddenly immense gulf of the living room, they both saw the door knob turn effortlessly. The door opened.

Three steps on the rug, and the tall man was standing there in the doorway, a gentle smile on his face, watching them. Noah wondered—

How come there's no blood on his suit?

They weren't moving now. Just standing there,

though Noah wanted to move, really wanted to, just as he wanted to call for his mother, out in the kitchen scrubbing plaster-like blotches of cornflakes from the breakfast dishes.

But all his mother heard was the unintelligible, high-pitched babble of the TV.

Sergeant Billy Rolson punched a button on his high-tech radio console and called for Barron to report in. He waited for an answer. Then he repeated his call.

"Damn," he said aloud, watched only by Willie Conway, about to be released from another night in the drunk tank. Where the hell could he be? he wondered. He hit a different button and called for DeFalco to answer. Even if he wasn't in his car, DeFalco would be carrying a radio around.

He waited, a crazy, disorienting feeling growing inside, making him feel dizzy.

"Christ," he whispered. "Where is everybody?" He pressed other buttons and ordered all available cars to get to the Reilly house. He repeated that message, hoping that DeFalco would finally break in and answer him.

When it was all over, he'd send someone to Schuyler Road to see what the hell could possibly be wrong with DeFalco's radio.

Sarah walked over to the man, even as Noah shook his head back and forth. She walked over to him, all the tension and fear gone from her face. The man placed a hand—

(The *same* hand, thought Noah)

—right around her waist, pulling her close. Noah tried to call out, to call for his daddy—

(He's not here. *Just like the dream.*)

—to call out for his mommy. To scream, so she'd stop the man.

But nothing happened.

The man tried to walk out the door, Sarah leaning into his side now.

Please let me scream, thought Noah.

Please.

"Ahhhggh." It died in his throat, a half-swallowed sound that somehow had been allowed to escape. Over the sound of running water, Julie heard it.

"Noah?" She turned the water off. "Noah, honey. You okay?" She dried her hands on a blue-checked dish rag and walked calmly through the great pool of morning sunlight in the dining room. "Is there something wrong. Can I . . ."

She entered the living room, and her life began to twist and turn before her eyes. Her first reaction was an absurd one, looking about the house to see what it looked like.

I would have picked up a bit, she thought, if I knew we were having . . .

Company.

The man smiled at her. She tried to ask, demand what he was doing here.

But the man simply reached down and touched Sarah's groin, and then traced a line up to her just-budding breasts. He watched Julie, as if curious about her reaction. Then, he turned to Noah, whose eyes were a deep, swollen red from crying.

Noah's face turned a bright, splotchy red. Sweat formed on his forehead and streamed down his face.

"No," Julie pleaded. "Not my baby, please leave my baby alone." Noah collapsed, sweat soaking his clothes, staining the pale rug.

She reached out to him, forcing her heavy hand to rise, to touch his forehead.

He was hot, his brain cooking at what had to be a temperature of over 105.

Five blocks away, a gaggle of sirens wailed, shifting to a higher pitch as they raced to Julie's house. The man looked perplexed, then amused. He guided Sarah out the front door, and down the steps to the sidewalk.

The door slammed behind him, a loud, sepulchral sound.

The police cars arrived, and Julie scooped up Noah, his eyes shut, lips cracked and dry.

"No, dear God. Please don't take my baby away from me."

She carried him, slippery in her arms, up the stairs, to the bathtub.

She turned the cold water on full and frantically laid the unconscious boy in the tub.

bushes for bits of fiber, looking for footprints in any dirt, dusting the doorknobs, futilely, for prints. They stopped frequently to drink from the Coleman water-cooler in the trunk of one of the cars.

At 2 p.m. Merrit was gone, called to look at something on Schuyler Road.

Finally, Jack went upstairs to sit on Noah's bed. He watched him breathe. It was labored, his small chest swelling while his dry lips opened to suck the air in.

Jack put his hand on the boy's forehead and felt the warmth that he had hoped would be gone.

"Daddy," Noah said, not even opening his eyes, "why do I have to be sick?"

"Everyone gets sick, champ. Your sister does, Mom does, and you know what it's like when I get sick."

"Yeah," said Noah flatly. "No fun."

"That's for sure. Being sick is no fun. But you'll be better soon, and we'll be up and . . ."

"Daddy, I don't feel like I'm going to get better."

Jesus, thought Jack. Give me a break.

"Please, Noah, you're going to be fine, real soon and we'll all . . ."

Noah's eyes blinked open, and Jack sensed the unasked question.

Sarah too? Will she be fine?

The phone rang, and Jack was eager to run into the bedroom and answer it. To escape. "Rest easy, guy. We're gonna be here with you, all the time."

Noah closed his eyes. Jack walked briskly into the bedroom. He picked up the phone on the night table.

Before he could speak, he heard Julie say, "Hello."
They had obviously picked up simultaneously.
There was a pause, a brief empty moment.

"Julie," said a man's voice. "I just heard the news
from one of the cops on the street down here. I feel
terrible. If there's any . . ."

Julie's voice seemed to catch in her throat, as if she
had trouble speaking. When she did talk it was a
quiet, almost whispery sound.

"You shouldn't have called, Patrick. Not now. Not
any more."

"But I was worried about you. I . . ."

"No," Julie said.

Another pause. Jack, a sickening feeling filling his
stomach, wondered whether Julie was looking over
her shoulder to see if he had come downstairs.

"No more, Patrick. No matter what happens, don't
call." Her voice became even quieter. "Let me have
my life back."

Then she hung up.

Jack stood there, the phone in his hand, the mute
button pressed down, and listened until Caldwell let
his phone clunk down into its cradle.

He walked downstairs.

A weird kind of giddiness seemed to settle on him,
a tremendous feeling of unreality. It's just too crazy,
he said. All of this is just not happening.

But every heavy-footed step down the stairs seemed
to confirm that, oh yes, it was very much happening.

He reached the living room, and made his way,
wraith-like, out to the kitchen.

"Who called?" he asked casually.

"Er . . . Joanne," Julie said, barely turning to look

255

at Jack, her face a bloated, puffy mess. "She heard about it and . . ."

Here Julie slowed down, each word coming out slowly, as if a tremendous effort was involved in its creation. She turned on the faucet to rinse out her cup.

"She said . . ."

"Sounded like a man's voice to me," Jack said, taking a sluggish step towards her. "Sounded like Patrick Caldwell calling to see how his girlfriend was doing." And here Jack reached out and let his hand close tightly over Julie's upper arm, spinning her around. "Who happens to be my wife."

She turned to him, the tears streaming down her cheeks, the words spilling out of her between gasps of breath. "I'm sorry," she sputtered out, as she brought her free hand up and pulled at her face. "I didn't want it to happen. It was just too much house, too much kids. . . ."

"And too much me," Jack said with a sneer.

"No," she moaned, shaking her head back and forth. "Not . . . you. It became a fantasy, my escape. The art show, the luncheons."

"The fucking."

"Oh, God, yes, maybe that too. But it's over, Jack. I lived with it and I ended it, and," Julie panted, trying to get it all out, "it's over."

She looked at Jack, his face hard, wearing cruel lines that she'd never seen before. "Please," she begged. "Forgive me."

And then she collapsed into him, howling out her anguish, and Jack's shirt became wet with her tears.

Gradually, she became quiet, and her whole body

was filled with a terrible dread of the first words he would say.

He grabbed Julie by the shoulders and pushed her away.

"Sometime," he said quietly, "when this is all over, you and I will go someplace and talk. But until then," Jack said fighting back his own tears, "we've got to stick together. 'Cause if we don't, I don't know what the hell is going to happen."

And they sat down, before a half-empty box of tissues, feeling the stillness of the afternoon.

The doorbell rang. Jack, in a fog, went to get it.

"Mr. Reilly, there's someone here who wants to see you." The rookie, somewhat recovered, gestured at a gray-haired man, dressed in rumpled pants and a suit jacket, standing at the barricade.

"No," Jack said hollowly. "We don't want to see anyone." He started to shut the door.

"He says it's important, Mr. Reilly. Something about . . . about your daughter."

Jack stopped. He looked at the man, hazily outlined in the sun's glare.

"Should I tell him to wait and talk to Captain Merrit?" the policeman asked, seeking confirmation of his judgment.

What did it matter? Jack thought. Was there any more pain to be felt, or more fear possible than that produced by the lurid, ghastly pictures inside their own heads? What could this old man say? That he'd seen Sarah dragged away in a car to nowhere, vanishing from their lives as if she never existed?

Just what could he tell them?

"No, it's okay," Jack said dully. "Let him come in.

But stay outside the door in case I want him out."

The cop seemed confused by Jack's answer, but he dutifully went to the barricade and told the man to go up to the front door.

The man walked slowly, Jack noticed, obviously suffering from the heat. He looked at least sixty, and his clothes were disheveled. Just don't be a crackpot, Jack threatened.

There's no telling what I might do to a crackpot.

Julie had gone upstairs to check Noah, sleeping naked in his bed, a cold face-cloth on his chest. She came down just as the old man arrived at the door.

He looked up at Jack, his lips trembling, searching for a word to say. His eyes scanned Jack's face, reading the suffering, the rage. Eyes filled with strength. He looked at Julie. So pretty, he'd think later. Just like the daughter.

"Mr. Reilly," he said, a trace of an accent. "My name is Eli Singer. And I think . . ." He paused, knowing the importance, the life-giving message of his words.

"I think I can save your daughter."

Jim Brooker pushed his lawn mower up a sharp incline, slashing the dandelion stalks and scattering the feathery seeds to the wind. He grunted, and thrust his belly against the hand controls to force the sticky, grass-clogged wheels to turn.

Mighty hot for a cook-out, he thought, passing the Char-Maid gas grill. But not too hot for the keg of beer sitting in the garage inside the old kiddie pool filled with ice.

Nope, not too hot for that at all.

Inside the house, Jim's wife Elaine was stabbing at their toilet bowl with a foam-tipped brush, scraping off weeks of near misses by Jim and their three sons. Elaine wondered why God couldn't have given her a daughter, someone nice and dainty. Someone to dress up, to go shopping with. Someone who sits to pee.

Most times Elaine felt like the maid at a rowdy logging camp. Feed them, clean up after them, listen to their loud talk about sports.

Yuck, as little Bill, their youngest, would say.

She flushed the toilet, and watched the bubbling bowl of water swirl away, to be replaced by more water.

Dirty brown water.

She frowned.

Elaine knew that their little community of Hudson Falls was special. It was an unincorporated chunk of land that belonged to no Westchester town or village, stuck in the middle between Harley and the northern villages of Croton, Cortland, and Yorktown Heights.

And she knew that their water quality tended, well, to vary. Hudson Falls had its own small reservoir system, a nearby lake that often ran dangerously low in summer. When that happened, the system was able to tap into a spur of the old aqueduct to get some fresh, clean water from upstate.

But this water looked like it had been sitting in someone's backyard for a week.

Well, never mind that, she thought, hearing Big Jim, as he liked to be called, shutting off his big red Lawn Boy. Now he'd probably pull out the pool, tap

259

the keg, and "test" it before setting up their mis-matched assortment of lawn furniture.

Elaine went into the kitchen, a shady room thanks to the fat old maple tree just outside the front door. The hamburgers and hot dogs were neatly lined up in metal trays inside the fridge, ready for Big Jim to do his chef routine. Oh, he was in his glory manning the grill, Elaine knew. While she waited in the background for it all to end so she could clean up.

You like it rare, Al? No problem, guy.

Elaine started to make a fresh pot of coffee. She dumped the left-over sludge from the day before and stuck the Faberware twelve-cup percolator under the faucet. She pulled back the lever for some cold, clear water.

It coughed, then sputtered, a misty sneeze hawking into the pot. Damn, she thought, what is wrong with this?

"Jim," she called, a high-pitched whine fine-tuned to the ears of the weekend handyman.

Then she heard a gurgle, and the sound of something coming up the pipe. Elaine relaxed, thinking that the water was on its way.

There was a loud thunk, then no sound at all. Something began to squeeze out of the spout. Elaine looked at it, mystified, disgusted, as some kind of transparent jelly began to drip out of the faucet. It formed a huge droplet and then plopped off into the pot. And another began forming. She turned the faucet off.

Now what in the world is this crap? she asked herself. *Now* how am I going to make coffee?

She touched her fingers to the goo. They began to

burn. Bad. It must be some kind of acid or something, she figured.

"Jim," she shouted. Then louder, "Jim!" She ran to the bathroom and wiped the stuff off her fingers, but the burning continued. She turned on the bathroom faucet and watched, horrified, as more of the jelly-goo dribbled out.

"Now we'll need a plumber for sure," she said to herself.

Outside, Big Jim was tasting the first bracing gulp of Genesee beer. He heard his wife screaming about something.

That's women for you, he thought. He headed indoors, beer in hand.

Merrit leaned into DeFalco's car, checking under the front seat, and on the floor in the back. The car radio seemed to be working fine. He noticed that DeFalco's walkie-talkie wasn't there.

"Okay," he said to the two cops, "show me the room." They walked across the street and around the side of the great white house, to the side door. They went downstairs.

"First thing we looked at, Captain, was this door." Merrit paused to run a hand along its smooth surface. The policemen looked embarrassed. "Then we smelled something."

They led the way down the narrow staircase. A single exposed bulb lit the basement. Merrit stood still and just looked at the floor.

Bingo, he thought.

He walked over to one of the shiny pools of deep

red. He touched it and brought a finger close to his nose. "Careful," he said quietly. "Be real careful when you step around. Where's the print?" One of the young cops pointed at a space near the heavy curtain.

Merrit stepped gingerly around the various pools until he was next to the red, waffle-shaped print. Cop shoes, he thought. "You've started blood tests?"

"Yes sir." Then, uncomfortably. "There seems to be at least three or four stains, some days old and completely dry."

"I can see that, officer," Merrit said with a smile. He looked up to his right. "That's the mirror?"

"Yes, sir. At least it looked like a mirror."

Merrit lifted the curtain, noting the iridescent colors that seemed to reflect off the strangely polished surface. Beveled, kind of, Merrit saw. It seemed to somehow absorb the light.

"Make sure fingerprints gets a look at this." He shook his head as he looked at the chair screwed to the ground. "Must've been a real sicko."

They went outside. Merrit heard the police radio calling for him. He trotted over to the car.

"Merrit here."

"Sergeant Rolson, Captain. We've got another missing person."

Shit, thought Merrit, this party just doesn't end.

"Go on."

"Someone named Mulcahy. Works for the Taconic State Park Commission. Some guy named Baker who works with him said he knew where he might be. Said Mulcahy was a bit drunk on Friday. He's been gone since."

"Where did he say he might be?"

"The aqueduct, Captain."

"Aqueduct? What the hell is that?"

Rolson explained about the old, abandoned water tunnel.

"Okay. Send some police to talk to this guy Baker. And send someone to look at this aqueduct."

The aqueduct, thought Merrit, a creepy feeling growing in his gut. A tunnel. A fucking tunnel that runs right to New York.

"Great," he said to himself.

Chapter 20

Jack opened the front door.

"Where is he?" Merrit asked. Jack gestured in the direction of the dining room.

Merrit walked quickly into the room.

Singer was sitting at the butcher-block table, his hands folded, waiting expectantly for Jack to come back. He looked tired, almost sick, Merrit thought. "C'mon, pal. If you have something to say, you can say it down at the police station." He turned to Jack. "I'm sorry they let him through."

Julie was in the kitchen, pouring two cups of tea. She walked into the dining room and handed one to Singer.

"I want to hear what he has to say. It can't hurt, Captain. Nothing can hurt." Her voice was final, absolute. She sat down. "Go on," she said to Singer.

Merrit leaned down and placed a strong hand on the rumpled old man's wrist. "Let's go, old fellow." Then, looking right at his eyes, "Leave these people alone."

"No!" Singer spat out. "No, they will hear me, and you will too. Look, look," he said digging his wallet out of his coat pocket. He fiddled a card out of a plastic window, a crumpled I.D. with a photo. "Dr. Eli Singer, Professor of Anthroplogy. And I was Head of the Department at the University of Berne. Until I resigned to do . . ."

He paused, licking a droplet of spittle off his lips. "To do this."

Merrit moved over to a free chair, his back to the open window. "And what is this thing that you do now, Dr. Singer?" Merrit scooped up the card and gave it a quick examination, then he passed it on to Jack.

"I've spent every day, *every day,* for the past five years trying to stop Ernst Kliber."

Merrit looked shocked. "Kliber? Where did you get that name from?"

Singer reached into his coat pocket and took out a vial of pills. He opened it, and popped a couple in his mouth. His face was flushed.

"When I first met Kliber he was seventeen. It was 1951 and he was my student. . . ."

Singer looked out the window, as if the past was out there. "Oh, yes, Ernst Kliber was a gifted researcher. Such an intellect, an absolutely uncanny ability to take parts of a scientific puzzle and use it to create a new thesis. He was a true 'wunderkind.'

"At that time I was just beginning my own work with the ancient civilizations of South America. My first expedition was scheduled for the winter of 1952. I invited Kliber to join my staff as a teacher assistant, with the possibility of joining the trip.

"At first I was not put off by his total pursuit of what he wanted. He had spent time in a state

266

orphanage during the war. Conditions were terrible. His family had been wiped out by Allied bombing. He was an ambitious, bitter young man. A hungry young man. Of course, he never let on how much he loathed me, how much he hated my 'Jewishness' as much as his own parents did. He handled whatever work I gave him, and I was impressed. No, more than that. I loved him for his genius."

Julie took a sip of her tea while Singer dug out a handkerchief and wiped his brow.

"Then, there were the expeditions and our tremendous discoveries. All reported, by the way, Captain, in your own *National Geographic*. My papers on the Mayan tombs caused a furor. There were cries of fraud, until I produced the documentary evidence . . . artifacts, photos, prints, all pointing to a civilization of such depth, and beauty, and yes, terror, to be absolutely overwhelming. But the most incredible discovery we kept secret."

Singer took a sip of his tea.

"Had enough, Julie? Can I get this crackpot out of here now?" Merrit said.

"No," she said quietly. "Go on, Dr. Singer."

"It was a parchment called the 'Xibalba,' the 'Other World.' People knew that certain Mayan sects had sacrificed people to the gods. Most often," he said quietly, "most often virgins. There was some speculation that it was just another primitive rite of spring, like that of the Bog people found in the fens of Denmark. It was just . . . speculation. The 'Xibalba,' though, told another story—of a civilization completely in the throes of powerful shamans, magicians who practiced a magic blacker and fouler

267

than any previously known. The parchment told how these shamans were able to contact another plane of existence. . . ."

"Oh, brother," Merrit groaned.

"A plane that was as distant as the ends of the universe, and as close as the air we breathe. It was a plane free from all time and space."

"And how was this plane reached?" Jack asked skeptically.

"Through the power of the mind," Singer said defiantly. "The special energy of the brain creates certain wave patterns, patterns that can open a door to this 'Other World.' We see visions, premonitions, and, of course, nightmares. The Mayan shamans discovered secrets of the brain, and secrets of light, that allowed them to do the impossible. The mirror in Kliber's basement is such a doorway."

"Sounds like TV to me," Merrit joked. No one laughed.

"The 'Xibalba' explained how to use fear and pain, it revealed certain secrets. But it wasn't until Kliber came upon the Sussex Manuscript in Edinburgh that he found the rest of the puzzle. From that moment he disappeared. Like others, he worked to summon something from that plane."

"Others?" Jack asked. "What others?"

Singer gave a deep sigh. "There's not time, Mr. Reilly. We must talk, make plans." Singer saw their faces, so totally unconvinced. He felt the first bitter taste of despair.

"Which culture would you like me to talk about? The Egyptian death cult that caused a whole city to be destroyed? Or maybe something closer to home, like the lost Roanoke colony. That was a case of their leader growing too friendly with the local Indians. If you see a wood carving found in that 'abandoned' colony it will live in your dreams. And then there's the Tunguska explosion. . . ."

"That I heard of," said Jack. "A big explosion, around the turn of the century. Some said it was a comet, maybe even a UFO."

"Nonsense. The explosion in the Tunguska Forest of Siberia was nothing less than an explosion of thermonuclear force. Life disappeared from an entire area, buildings were destroyed, trees uprooted. The seismic wave traveled around the planet twice. Forty miles away, people were knocked down by the force.

"You see, a primitive cult, with roots in the barbaric tribes of pre-Christian Russia, had tried to capture something from another plane. But such a thing cannot stay here. It's like a creation formed of antimatter. It must return to its own world. But if it were to create offspring here, they could stay. Forever."

"Okay," Merrit announced. "That's enough for me. I don't know why we listened to this garbage," he said to Jack, "but I can promise you that we don't have to listen to anymore."

The door bell rang. "Wait here," Merrit ordered Singer. He went with Jack to the front door. "Probably the next nutcase."

Julie looked at the old man. He was tired, defeated, caved in. "They must believe me," he begged. "We may still be able to save your daughter. She's still alive. She's been . . . selected for this night. But we must act soon. I have a plan that might save her."

269

Then, his voice became almost a whisper. "It might save us all."

Jack and Merrit entered the room slowly. Jack's pupils had shrunk to fine-pointed dots. Merrit rubbed his chin, and looked at Singer.

"That was the desk sergeant. Two of our people have disappeared into the aqueduct. They don't answer their radio."

Singer looked up, a trace of hope in his eyes.

"And," Merrit said with difficulty, "before they went in they reported seeing footprints in a muddy section near the tunnel. Prints of bare feet. Child's prints."

Julie started sobbing.

"And," Merrit said slowly, "another pair of prints. Each a yard long, split down the middle, with two claws that dug right into the muck." He paused. "They were right next to the footprints."

Merrit sat down heavily, as Jack went over beside Julie. For a moment, nobody said anything.

"Okay, Professor," Merrit said. "Keep talking to us."

Chapter 21

It was dusk. The endless outpouring of heat during the day had stopped. A small breeze gently shook the graceful mimosa and tickled the fat leaves of the maple trees.

Sunday night, and many people were sitting out on their porch, some talking about the terrible, terrible things happening in the town, others carrying on the time-honored debate over the relative merits of the Mets and the Yankees.

The steady whine of air conditioners competed with the more insistent rattling of the cicadas.

A hot summer night in July. And for the people in Harley, the most important night in their lives.

Merrit got out of his car and walked briskly over to Allan Smith.

"Thanks, Allan. I appreciate your volunteering."

"No problem, Captain. Are you sure you want me to wait over here . . . so far away from the door?"

Merrit looked uneasy. "Yes. Whatever happens, don't come down to the basement. Just buzz me once on the radio if anyone, or anything, starts coming in."

"Any*thing?*" Smith asked.

Merrit smiled. "No questions, Allan. Not, at any rate, till this is all over."

Smith walked away from the door to Kliber's house and stood off to the side, near the thick hedges. Three houses down some children were using the last dull light of evening to swing back and forth, while lightning bugs blinked around them.

Merrit entered the house, and walked downstairs.

So quiet, he thought. When he stopped moving in the basement there was no sound, and he wished he could have Smith down here, standing right by his side, his Colt .44 Service revolver in his hand.

He lit a cigarette, noting the curious way the smell of the smoke mingled with other danker odors.

Damn glad I'm a smoker tonight, he thought.

He patted his side pocket, checking for his extra pack of Camel Lights. He wondered whether he might get hungry later. Then he looked around the room, the mad swirl of red still visible on the floor.

Nope. Hunger would not be a problem.

Was he crazy? he asked himself. Crazy to believe Singer's story? Crazy to believe some rookie's report of a footprint?

Too bad the cop wasn't around to answer a few questions. But like lots of people in this town, he had gotten the "disappearing disease." Here today . . .

But it was his frustration that made Merrit agree to the plan. What else could he do? Send a platoon of cops into the aqueduct? A possible option. If you knew what you were sending them down for. Or maybe put a description of Kliber on the wire services, have it plastered on the front page of every newspaper in the country.

Have you seen this man? He collects people.

But by tomorrow, Singer had told them with chilling finality, it would be too late. Imagine an express path to New York City, the Big Apple, filled with millions of people, many out in the streets escaping from the city heat.

Hot town. Summer in the city.

And imagine, Singer said with a look that made Merrit's stomach heave, imagine them all massacred like a human ant colony crushed into dust.

Merrit felt for the hammer hanging off his belt, a heavy, three-pound mallet that could put a good-sized dent in just about anything. And it could, of course, crack a mirror, then smash it into millions of pieces.

He looked at his watch. In fifteen minutes they'd be at the aqueduct. They'd tell him to uncover the mirror. He'd wait. Then he'd crack it, just a little bit.

And he'd wait some more. For Kliber, maybe, or, if Singer was right, something else.

His heart was beating fast, and his skin was prickled from the coolish air and his own—what would he call it? Fear.

He thought of Singer's final words, repeated for he fourth or fifth time.

Don't look at the mirror.

Merrit reached down and turned on his radio, letting its high-pitched hiss end the silence.

"Rolson, are you there?"

Rolson answered immediately.

273

Merrit continued. "Double check all the police along the route. Remind them to take no action other than to keep citizens out of the way." Merrit heard Rolson acknowledge. Leaving the radio on, Merrit put it in his back pants pocket.

Outside, a car roared by, windows open, radio blasting.

Merrit waited.

Jack helped Singer climb up the slope to the grassy ridge of the aqueduct. James Baker was already there, waiting for them.

"You know," Baker said quietly to Jack, "I don't think it's such a good idea for the old fellow to go down there. The ladder's kinda small and slippery, and the footing's not so good."

"I'm fine!" Singer said sharply, pulling himself up to Jack and then, with a great deal of effort, stepping up to the ridge. "I'll . . . be," he panted, "just fine."

Baker raised his eyebrows.

Ahead, two policemen stood around the grating, talking quietly. They turned and watched the three men walk up to them.

"Evening," one of the cops said. "Is . . ."

"You cannot stand here," Singer snapped. "You must," he looked around, "wait over there. And don't let anyone near this hole."

The cops smirked at each other.

Reilly took his radio and turned it on. Singer started to strap on a hard hat with a lantern.

"Captain. We're about to go in," Jack said. The

cops straightened up and backed away.

"Fine," Merrit answered. "I'm all set here."

"C'mon, c'mon," Singer said, looking up at the sky. "We must go now."

"Okay," Baker said. He leaned over and grabbed the grating with his hands. With a tremendous grunt, he lifted it off. "Damn, that's heavy."

He looked at Singer, who was already moving to the narrow metal ladder. "If you want, I'll go in with you guys."

Singer paused. "No. Thank you, but go home, Mr. Baker, to your family. Go home, and stay there."

Baker shrugged as Singer disappeared. "Watch that old guy," he said to Jack. "Keep him away from that webbing shit."

"Sure," Jack said. "And thanks."

Then Baker watched Jack vanish down the hole.

They were together, Noah and Julie, lying on the king-sized bed. Julie had fixed some popcorn in the microwave as a treat for Noah, but he had refused it.

Of course, they didn't talk about the morning. Noah's fever had dropped down to a manageable level, but he was still weak, pale, and wanted to just lie next to his Mommy.

The bedroom TV was on. They were watching the Sunday Night Disney Movie. Tonight, it was about a family that moves into a, ha-ha, haunted house. The father sold novelty items—masks, magic tricks, and gags—and the first ten minutes of the film consisted of his terrorizing his family with plastic vomit and hand buzzers.

Julie went to shut it off.

"No," Noah said.

So she left it on, laughing too loudly at the father's strange masks and goofy tricks. Trying to talk to Noah, distracting him when the real ghosts came on.

But every five minutes Julie prayed for Jack to come back, banging open the door like Robert Young returning from a day's work at God-knows-what, and say . . .

Here she is, Mother. I found our little girl! Now, what's for dinner?

Jack turned his lantern on, letting it blend with Singer's, cutting out matching ovals of yellow.

He wanted to leave.

He fumbled for the radio, nervous like a kid on his first date.

First time, huh, kid?

Jack spoke into the radio. "Merrit, we're inside now."

"Okay," Merrit answered. "Do you see anything?"

"Yes. I see—"

Bubbles. Great, soccer-ball-sized bubbles lining the wall. Looking just like the eye of a housefly. You know, enlarged maybe one thousand times. Or maybe the bubbly drool made by a spittle bug.

"—eggs," Jack said. "The tunnel is filled with, I don't know. They look like frog eggs."

"Stop talking!" Singer ordered. "We must be quiet. Tell him that we will let him know when we're ready. Tell him not to call us."

Singer reached into his pocket for some kind o

276

book. A black book, with gilt edges that caught the light.

There was a sound.

"You hear that?" Jack asked. To his left, he thought he saw something move inside the milky bubbles. He stared hard at one, and figured that it must have simply been the play of the light.

"For what it's worth," Jack whispered. "I believe you. The whole story."

They started their walk down the tunnel.

Chapter 22

They splashed through the water, only now becoming aware of the incredible smell that filled the tunnel. For Jack, it reminded him of when he and Julie had bought an old, wind-up phonograph, a handsome, near-mint-condition record player from the 1920s.

It was a big machine, a Brunswick, standing five feet tall, with large cabinets in the bottom for record storage. They polished up the outside and, with records picked up at the same tag sale, tested out state-of-the-art hi-fi, circa 1929. While the Mozart sounded a bit too tinny for modern ears, the machine was perfect for "Aye, Aye, Aye" sung by the Four Caballeros.

Then Julie and he became aware of this horrible odor that filled their living room. And the only thing new was, of course, the Brunswick.

Jack figured that maybe there was something inside the cabinet. He had gone for a flashlight to look inside it.

As Julie hovered behind him, reluctantly peering into the cabinet's shadows, Jack reached in and pulled out a stiff, fat old mole, all curled up and sticky like an old piece of taffy.

Somehow they never felt that great about the phonograph after that.

Singer, too, knew the smell. He knew it the way you knew your own sweat smell after a hot day, or the musty odor of a cluttered closet.

How could he forget, after all, the smell of that first Mayan tomb, the preserved corpses of bodies a millennia old, neatly chopped into pieces, wrapped, ready to be served?

But it wasn't the smell of the cloth and the chemicals that filled his brain with nightmares.

It was another smell, a ripe, unbelievable foulness that seemed to fill the tomb though it had been sealed for centuries. The smell was alive, present. *Lingering*. A horrible, gut-wrenching odor that left a sickening taste on his tongue.

The same smell, Singer knew, that he was breathing in now.

The floor around Merrit was littered with his butts, all smoked down to that last few millimeters before being chucked away.

There was enough smoke in the room to make his eyes water.

"Captain Merrit?"

He heard Jack's voice, sounding distant and hollow. "Yes, Jack," Merrit said wondering what the two dozen policemen listening to this craziness made of it all. Not to mention all CB fans and police-radio buffs eavesdropping.

"Captain," Jack said quietly, "we've seen nothing so far." The voice was tremulous, thought Merrit. Scared. You're over your head, boy. You should have let me go with the old professor. You should have . . .

"The egg-things just seem to go down the whole length of the aqueduct. It's incredible."

"And Baker's webbing?" Merrit asked. "Any sign of that?"

"If there's any webbing, it's just gone, or hidden by the other stuff." Merrit heard Singer tell Jack to hurry up and be quiet.

"Okay. We're going to leave our radio on so you can hear anything. I got it in my hand so you'll hear me tell you when to start."

Yeah, Merrit thought. When to take his hammer and give the mirror just the smallest little smash, just enough to . . .

"Keep it covered until we tell you to take the curtain off," Singer said. "And don't . . ."

"I know, I know," Merrit laughed. "Don't look at it."

Or I'll turn to stone.

"We gotta see something soon," Jack said. "He has to be just ahead."

"Good luck," Merrit said softly.

He heard their splashing steps on his radio.

"Wait!" Singer hissed. "I hear something."

Jack listened, but all he could hear was Singer's labored breathing.

"There! Don't you hear it? Steps, and water."

And Jack heard it. Oh yes, he heard it. Something

moving around, making small sounds in the filmy water. Maybe it was even Sarah, wandering around, waiting for them. . . .

"He must hear us," Singer whispered. "He must know we're here. But," he gasped, swallowing his breath, "he probably doesn't care." Singer paused. "He wants us to come. Step slowly now, Jack. We must not be surprised by him. And use your ears. They must be better than mine."

They kept moving.

Merrit heard Jack and Singer talking, picking up just bits and pieces of Singer's whispered words. That they had seen or heard something was clear.

And, thought Merrit, they had, in the excitement, probably forgotten to tell him to take the curtain off and get ready.

He walked to the wall-sized curtain and pulled idown. The massive mirror was exposed.

Merrit reached into his belt and slid out the heavy claw-shaped hammer.

There was a good ghost and a bad ghost in thmovie.

The good ghost was a mother who wanted to geher little boy back from a man who kept hirimprisoned inside a many-gabled mansion.

The bad ghost was the man, his face eaten away ba terrible fire that left his mansion a burning hull

Noah didn't complain when Julie turned it off. Hjust closed his eyes and cuddled tightly against h

mother, while Julie ran her hand, over and over, through the ultra-fine corn silk of his hair.

They saw the bodies, like a gallery of specimens from a human museum. They saw the two policemen who had first entered the aqueduct, and then other people, all strangers, all now exposed in the icy intimacy of death.

The people—a few men, some women, a small black boy—were without clothes, their puffy bodies somehow weaved into the bulbous honeycomb on the walls.

"Oh, God," Jack groaned. "I don't know if I can handle this, Singer. I feel like I'm going to be sick."

"Stop it! Don't look at them. They're dead, Mr. Reilly. Dead. But your daughter is still alive. *Still alive.* If you can't go on, I'll have to do it by myself." Then, he added slowly, "And I'm not too sure I'm strong enough."

Jack heard a splash.

A loud "ker-plunk" that couldn't be more than 100 feet from them. Then, a slithering sound, like an alligator flinging itself into a swamp.

"Jesus," Jack said. "That's close."

"He's just waiting, Jack. Somewhere down there. Just . . . waiting."

"Let's go," Jack said hoarsely.

Yeah, Jack thought. Let's go kill the fucker.

Sort of pretty, Merrit thought.

I mean, it's obviously not a mirror. Barely reflects any light at all. Sort of gives off its own light. So many shades of blue, and red, and orange.

Why, it seems almost to move, to swirl, and the longer he looked at it, the more it moved.

He best turn away, he thought. Like Dr. Singer told him to.

He kept on watching.

Chapter 23

"My light!" Singer said, his voice suddenly apprehensive. His lantern's light had shrunk to a pale yellow and then died completely.

"Shit," Jack said. "Let me see." He took Singer's hat and gave the light a bang. It stirred somewhat to a dull glow and then was gone. "But it's a new battery, they said," Jack yelled. "What the hell happened to it?"

"The moisture," Singer offered. "Maybe a loose wire, maybe . . ."

"Something else," Kliber said.

Jack turned, startled into dropping the helmet. Kliber looked like some kind of mountain climber, dressed in a blue sweater and coarse gray slacks. His rubber boots went to his knees.

"Kliber," Singer whispered, sounding weak.

And then, from the shadows, still dressed in a short nightie, Sarah appeared, walking bare-footed through the water to stand next to Kliber.

"You god-damn—" Jack screamed, starting for Kliber.

Singer quickly grabbed his arm. "No!"

285

Kliber smiled, a warm, generous grin of triumph. He gave Sarah's taut body a familiar squeeze.

And then, letting his arm drop, he changed.

Jack's light caught the sudden transformation in only bits and pieces.

Kliber's skull seemed to twist around, and then swell like a blister, before elongating into a dull-eyed, almost eel-shaped head.

Jack looked at the arm.

It had been replaced with something that resembled a kind of carnivorous plant, with dripping, gleaming tendrils and teeth.

And there were the feet, clumsily shaped, two-part claws that curled and uncurled with a crazy anticipation.

Jack was moaning, mumbling, as he backed further away. His daughter, suddenly a foreign thing to him, stood there, lovingly beside the thing that towered over her.

"Come back!" Singer begged Jack. "I . . . I can't see. I need you."

The words penetrated Jack's skull. Stop. Come back. I need you. And somehow Jack did stop, shaking and quivering in the water, his pee running down his leg.

"The radio," Singer said. "The radio!"

Now, at last, Jack came back from the abyss.

"Merrit!" Jack screamed. "Take the curtain off."

He ran beside Singer, even as the creature took a leaden step forward.

Singer held his book high, and began to repeat a mumbled phrase over and over, a string of gibberish that sounded like a baby's drivel to Jack. Over and over, Singer said the words. While the creature, now no more than five yards away, plopped towards them. Singer stepped next to Jack as he kept his bizarre litany going.

To the side, there was a fluttering inside one of the egg cases, a fluttering that made Jack lean into Singer's body.

Then Singer shouted.

"You've been tricked, Shub-Niggurath! Tricked. Even now Kliber is having your portal destroyed, trapping you here, destroying you."

It stopped, as if considering this even more foreign language, translating the words into an idea. A feeling.

"Yes. Trapped. Destroyed. Like the others."

And now the jelly-like eyes of the thing seemed to glint in the light. It raised an arm, letting its teeth open, and sound emerged.

Something guttural, the sound of wind racing down a deserted alley.

"Now," Singer whispered. "Tell Merrit *now*."

Jack brought the radio right up to his mouth, making sure that it was on.

"Merrit!" he said, his voice high-pitched and totally distorted by fear. "Hit the mirror now."

The creature turned its head as if reading some kind of message in the dank tunnel air. Singer and Jack stood just a few feet away.

"Merrit!" Jack screamed. "Hit it. Hit the mirror now, for Christ's sake."

The radio was silent, other voices banned from speaking on the line no matter what. The hiss of the radio was now met by an expectant gurgle from the head of the creature.

It grabbed Singer.

"No!" he screamed.

Jack's light caught the man's glasses tumbling off to the side.

It brought the old man up to its head, where it opened its mouth and dug a four-inch hole right through his chest. Then it threw Singer against the wall, letting the old man stick to the egg-shaped things, joining the human gallery.

Jack was alone now.

All by his lonesome.

He tried to think, really tried to think, but he was frozen with fear.

What next? he asked himself. What was ready to spring from all those glistening bubbles, even now swirling around ready to just pop out? And what are the bodies down here for? do you suppose.

But he knew those answers. Sure he did. But what . . . what would Sarah do, helping it prepare for the moment when all the eggs would open?

Jack ran. He heard the creature just behind him, a loping movement, effortless, fast. He knew that it was hopeless but he had to keep running, had to keep trying.

Smith heard the radio. He heard it and he tried to ignore it.

His orders were clear. He was not to move and he was not to go into the basement.

No matter what.

But there was a time for orders to be ignored, h

thought. And he hoped that this was one of them.

He ran downstairs, knowing that his future was on the line.

"Captain, is everything okay down—"

He saw Merrit. He was standing right in front of the mirror, right in front of a twelve-foot tall, three-dimensional picture of the craziest fucking place Smith had ever seen.

And Merrit looked like he was about to walk in.

Smith ran over to him, and pulled him away, back from the mirror.

"Captain! Captain Merrit! Pull out of it. Are you okay?"

He had turned Merrit's face away from the mirror, training his own dark brown eyes on Merrit's. Slowly, almost reluctantly, Merrit snapped out of his stupor.

"What . . . What happened? And what are you doing down here? I told you . . ."

"Yes, sir, but they *called* for you, told you to hit the mirror. And I found you walking into the thing. Like some kind of zombie."

"Oh, Jesus," Merrit said and he reached for his radio. "Jack, Jack come in."

There was no answer.

"Jack! Jack, what's going on?"

There was hiss. Then, finally, a panting voice.

"Break the mirror," he gasped. "Break it."

Merrit looked around for his hammer, and saw it on the ground. He picked it up and brought it against the polished surface, keeping his eyes turned away. "Don't look at it," he ordered Smith.

The first blow did nothing.

"Damn," he said. And he pulled back and let go with more force.

A crack appeared.

Jack stopped, letting the radio fall.

The creature reached out for him.

"Now the doorway is broken," Jack said quickly. "See? You are being trapped by Kliber. He . . ." Jack searched for something convincing to say. "He wants all your power."

From the radio on the ground, Jack thought he heard something.

But it was the creature that reacted. It staggered back as if hearing some tremendous thunderclap roaring around it.

"It will be all gone," Jack said. "And you will be destroyed. Unless . . ."

(God, make this fucker believe me.)

"Unless you go back now, before it's too late."

From within the creature's body there came a terrible wrenching sound. Like some kind of diseased tissue, some human pus, Kliber slipped through the skin, tumbling from the creature's chest like an unwanted newborn.

Kliber seemed startled. Jack backed away, moving as fast as he could without running, trying to get past the open grate.

He hoped that there were no cops standing beside it. For their sake.

Kliber stood up, a loathing on his face that Jack could feel.

Jack kept backing away. He heard Kliber speaking

290

to the creature.

More gibberish.

Kliber raised his hands and made some kind of sign.

The creature raised its arms to Kliber, moved them close to his shoulders, and ripped his body in half. There had been no time for a scream.

And that, thought Jack, is the end of that partnership.

Chapter 24

Jack ran past the tunnel opening and waited, shivering, praying that it would go straight out, ignoring him. He shut his eyes, and turned off his lantern.

It came, a terrible, high-pitched squeal coming right at him. Then Jack smelled it as he saw a dark hulk claw its way out of the aqueduct.

It was gone. He quickly turned on his light.

"Sarah!" Jack yelled, running back down the foul tube. Then, louder . . .

"Sarah!"

Small sounds escaped from the glistening egg cases.

He ran, his adrenaline kicking in.

Tiny, noisy fissures opened in the eggs. Jack heard an oozing, dripping sound. Clumps of jelly-stuff fell from the ceiling.

"Sarah!" And he saw her, sitting down in the muck, her legs scratched and dirty. Jack slowed. He knew that special fear only given to a parent who has lost a child to someone.

(Are you still my daughter?)

She looked up at him, glassy-eyed, her hair wet and matted with dirt.

She started crying, and she raised her arms to him. "Daddy."

Jack went to her, scooped her up off the tunnel floor.

A glob of jelly landed on his bare arm, burning it. He shook it off.

He walked as fast as he could, carrying her close to his chest. Sarah was crying, a small, helpless whimpering that she buried in his shoulder.

"It's okay now, honey. It's all over." He paused not quite believing it himself.

"Everything's going to be okay."

The radio was silent. Merrit had no way of knowing whether he had been too late, whether everything went according to plan.

The old man's plan.

He had heard Jack talking, then someone, in the distance, screaming. Had he been in time?

They waited, he and Smith, in the corner, their backs to the mirror, the mirror now radiating a funny kind of heat. Merrit swore that he could smell things, strange, disgusting. . . .

He heard a sound.

A high-pitched squeal.

The sound of panic, thought Merrit. He tightened his sweaty grip on the hammer.

"I think . . ." Smith began, but Merrit shushed him.

The squeal got louder, then it was at the doorway,

a mad siren hurting their ears. They heard something big flopping down the stairs.

Merrit risked a sideways glance. "Jesus," he whispered, knowing that he'd just seen something that would live forever in his nightmares.

It went directly for the mirror. Merrit didn't move, but he let himself watch its curved back, watch it step up to the mirror and scream one final time before raising an arm and . . .

Stepping in.

"Now!" yelled Merrit, and he swung around, forcing his eyes to look down, up, left, or right. Anywhere but straight ahead. He used the chair to gauge how close he was.

Wouldn't want to trip now, he thought.

He pulled back with the hammer as far as he could, and then let go with the strongest, most desperate swing of his life. At that moment, he had to look at the mirror.

It was watching him. No, not just watching him, it was reaching for him, starting to reach out and pull him in to that terrible place.

Too late, pal, Merrit thought.

The hammer hit, and the mirror shivered and finally collapsed into a thousand heavy, dull pieces, scattered around his feet, filling the basement with a crystalline roar that went on for unbearable seconds.

They stood there, in silence, for a few minutes. The air was still redolent of the creature and its world.

"Get some cops in here to sweep this mess up. Have them bag it and then take it to wherever it can be incinerated." Merrit started for the door, then stopped. "And Smith, thanks. Thanks a lot."

Later, all the shards would be swept up, bagged, and melted down, just as Merrit had ordered.

All the shards, except for one small piece pocketed as a souvenir by one of the cops.

Jack held his daughter up so that the police at the opening could grab her arms and help her out.

They tried to pull her out gently. She emerged to see a small crowd of Harley and State police gathered around. Jack climbed out, and was embarrassed for his daughter, for her exposed, disheveled condition.

A dazed expression was on most of the faces watching him.

"Where's a car?" Jack yelled.

"A state trooper stepped forward. "I . . . I have my patrol car over there," he said, pointing to a nearby corner.

"Could you take us home?" Jack asked as he again picked up Sarah.

The trooper led them away. Gradually, the crowd broke up and left the aqueduct.

Epilogue

It was late August, the time when people begin to remember that summer must eventually end. Each night it grew a bit darker, a bit earlier, and the occasional cool morning was a sad reminder of the cold days to come.

These were the weekends when families tried to squeeze in all the things that they had hoped to do all through the summer. A big trek to Jones Beach to get that "lobster look" before going back to work on Monday. A twi-night double-header at Yankee Stadium in the home-stretch run for a pennant. A trip to Playland.

Playland, perched on Long Island Sound in the upscale town of Rye, was one of a dying breed of amusement parks. Owned and operated by Westchester County, the park was spotlessly clean, filled with freshly painted art-deco filigree, classic rides, and an adjacent beach. A lot of things seemed to have gone down the tubes, people would say, but somehow, miraculously, Playland had stayed real *nice*.

Jack was enjoying himself. While Sarah was a bit

old to fully enjoy the park as a family thing (she'd much rather be running around with her friends), Noah was in heaven, jumping up and down from excitement, consuming ride tickets and cotton candy with equal regularity.

Jack held Julie close as they walked down the large, shrub-lined promenade that went through the middle of the park.

"Daddy, can I go on the Dragon Coaster?" Noah begged. "Please!" They were just next to the impressive coaster, close enough to hear the screams of its wide-eyed passengers as it plummeted down, into the mouth of the dragon.

Jack smiled. He knew that Noah was too small.

"Go check your height against the height-line, champ. If you're tall enough, I'll take you on the ride." Noah dashed away.

"Daddy," Sarah said petulantly, "you know he's too short."

Jack laughed. "Sure. But let him check that himself. I don't want to give him the bad news." Noah walked back to them, disappointed. "Hey, there's bumper cars ahead," Jack offered. "We can go on them."

"Okay," Noah said.

They walked on. It was all receding, thought Jack. The children's nightmares (not to mention his own), the impromptu crying jags, the tossing and turning at night, twisting the bed sheet into a thick rope.

Life was almost normal again.

Almost.

Of course, it helped that he had stopped his reading. For a while, Jack was devouring books on clairvoyance, astral projection, telekinesis, the spirit world, whatever. If it was strange, he read about it. He read enough to learn that Singer hadn't told him everything. He read about things that made him double-lock the front door at night and never, ever skip church on Sunday.

But Julie had laid down the law.

With Sarah still on edge, the books had to go. Even the titles were disturbing her. So Jack hauled the carton of slightly used books back to his store.

He felt good that the Taconic Park Commission had sealed off the aqueduct, even if all the webbing and the other things seemed to rot away only a few days after that night.

It was over, he kept telling himself.

Now if only he could believe it.

"Oh, look!" Noah squealed. "Mystery Manor! Can we go in, Dad, huh?"

Outside the building a coterie of crudely painted skeletons, witches, and goblins prowled a day-glo graveyard. The obligatory cackling laugh filled the air. The "Manor" was a walk-through, and they watched some excited Latino teenagers enter.

"I don't know, champ. I . . ."

"Aw, c'mon Dad," Sarah said, mediating. "I'll go in with him. You guys can wait for us here."

Jack looked at Julie. "I guess so," she said, picking up the ball Jack passed to her. Then, to Sarah, she said, "But stay with your brother. I don't want him running around in there."

"Yipeee!" Noah said, pulling Sarah away. Jack

quickly stuck the last ten tickets in her hand.

The kids waved as they went in the oddly tilted door.

Jack and Julie sat down on the bench, both feeling like an old married couple.

"Having fun?" Jack asked.

Julie smiled. "Yes. You know how I'm a sucker for amusement parks. You?"

"Oh, sure. It's great," he said without a good deal of conviction.

(It's never far from our thoughts, is it? he asked himself. It's always right there.)

They leaned back on the bench, resting their tired feet, happy to just sit and wait.

The group of teenagers came bounding out of the Manor, talking excitedly in Spanish, the heavily made-up girls looking coy.

"Probably a good place to make out," Jack said.

Then another group of kids came out, laughing, young kids that had gone in after Noah and Sarah. Jack sat up a bit, watching the exit door. More children came out. Jack stood up.

"Jack? Jack, what's wrong?"

"They haven't come out. Everyone . . . everyone else after them has come out. They're still in there." He went over to the pimply ticket-taker.

"Jack," Julie called out to him, her heart beginning to beat fast, faster.

The kid listened to Jack, and shrugged.

"You need a ticket."

The ticket booth was way down near the park entrance, Jack knew.

"My kids are in there. I'm going in," he said flatly

300

He pushed the kid out of the way and ran up a wood
ramp to the door.

He opened the door. A gust of air was blown in hi:
face. More screaming, inside now, echoed from a tape
loop. He walked in the near-dark, moving across a
bridge that wobbled back and forth.

"Noah! Sarah!" he yelled.

He moved on. A skeleton popped out of a grave
with a pneumatic whoosh, startling Jack. "Noah!"
he yelled.

"Da . . . Daddy." The sound was close.

Jack ran now, bumping into a wall, feeling
feathery, spidery things running through his hair.
He came to Noah, curled up in the shadows, crying.
Jack picked him up.

"Where's Sarah." Noah kept crying. "Where's
Sarah!" Jack commanded.

"In there," Noah sniveled. "In the mirrors."

Jack moaned, and he ran with Noah, into the nex
room.

It was a mirror maze, with six-foot mirrors tilted a
crazy angles. Jack used his elbow to find his way
through, banging left and right, testing what was
mirror, what was path, and then yelling out Sarah's
name.

He saw her.

Standing in a cul-de-sac of five or six mirrors.
There were dozens of Sarahs standing there, all with
their two hands up to the mirror, touching it.

"Sarah," Jack said gently. Then, letting Noah
slide down to the ground, he put an arm around her.

She wasn't crying, but her eyes had a deep, dry
sadness that chilled Jack.

"I thought . . ." she said slowly. Then, looking at her father, "I thought of Shelly, and the others."

"Yes," Jack said softly, and he guided her out, letting Noah take her hand, out to the entrance. They passed some girls giggling their way in.

When they got out, Julie was standing there, waiting for them. She ran over, pushing aside the security guards, and encircled them with her strong arms.

The ticket-taker watched them as they walked away.